Oxford University Press, Walton Street, Oxford OX2 6DP

Oxford London
New York Toronto Melbourne Auckland
Kuala Lumpur Singapore Hong Kong Tokyo
Delhi Bombay Calcutta Madras Karachi
Nairobi Dar es Salaam Cape Town

and associated companies in
Beirut Berlin Ibadan Mexico City Nicosia

Oxford is a trade mark of Oxford University Press

© Charles Keeping 1984
First published 1984

British Library Cataloguing in Publication Data
Keeping, Charles
Sammy Streetsinger.
I. Title
823'.914 J PZ7
ISBN 0-19-279782-4

Phototypeset by Tradespools Ltd, Frome, Somerset
Printed in Hong Kong

Sammy Streetsinger

Charles Keeping

Oxford University Press

OXFORD TORONTO MELBOURNE

The city has a bypass, and the bypass has a subway beneath it. Most days you will find Sammy Streetsinger there, dancing and singing to his one-man band for coins from the generous people who use the subway to cross the road.

Children and animals love to dance with him, and he is very happy here, because he remembers the time he left the subway to seek fame and fortune. This is how it happened . . .

One day, the Big Chance Circus came to town. Ivor Chance,
the ringmaster, needed a fresh act and saw Sammy in the subway.
He had a sly idea.

He hugged him like an old friend, and flattered him, and invited
him to join the circus. Sammy, being a simple soul, was easily
fooled. Thoughts of sweet success crossed his innocent mind; so
he joined the travelling troupe, leaving his friends and the subway
behind.

Each night, Sammy was dressed up as a clown, and performed his usual act in the sawdust ring. He loved the crowds and applause, and dreamed of the fame he would achieve one day.

But Ivor Chance had other ideas. He really wanted a fool, an idiot.
One night, while Sammy was performing and showing off, Ivor
had a hook lowered from the big top. The hook caught in Sammy's
trousers and hauled him high into the dome and left him dangling.

Soon his trousers came off, and he fell down onto the sawdust ring.

Water was squirted over him and the crowd roared with laughter as he sat cold, wet, and trouserless. All alone. Poor Sammy, he was so disillusioned. He felt completely humiliated.

Now in the audience that night was Mr Biggknob, an impresario. He came to see Sammy after the show and whispered, 'Do you always want to be the guy who loses his pants for laughs? Get wise. Let me handle your career. I'll make you into a real entertainer.' 'Oh, yes please, sir,' cried Sammy. And again he dreamed of fame and wealth, his name up in lights.

Soon he was billed at the 'Palace of Dreams' in the city centre, but in a totally different disguise.

With his hair ironed and frizzed up, a guitar and a gaudy suit, he was soon singing on stage each night with two gyrating girls. The crowds went wild with delight, though they could hardly hear him above the amplified music.

It wasn't long before he was topping the bill at the Stadium.

But slowly it seemed he was losing touch with the audience.
He was tiny in this vast hall, and could only hear them screaming out there in the darkness. They didn't seem to be hearing him at all.

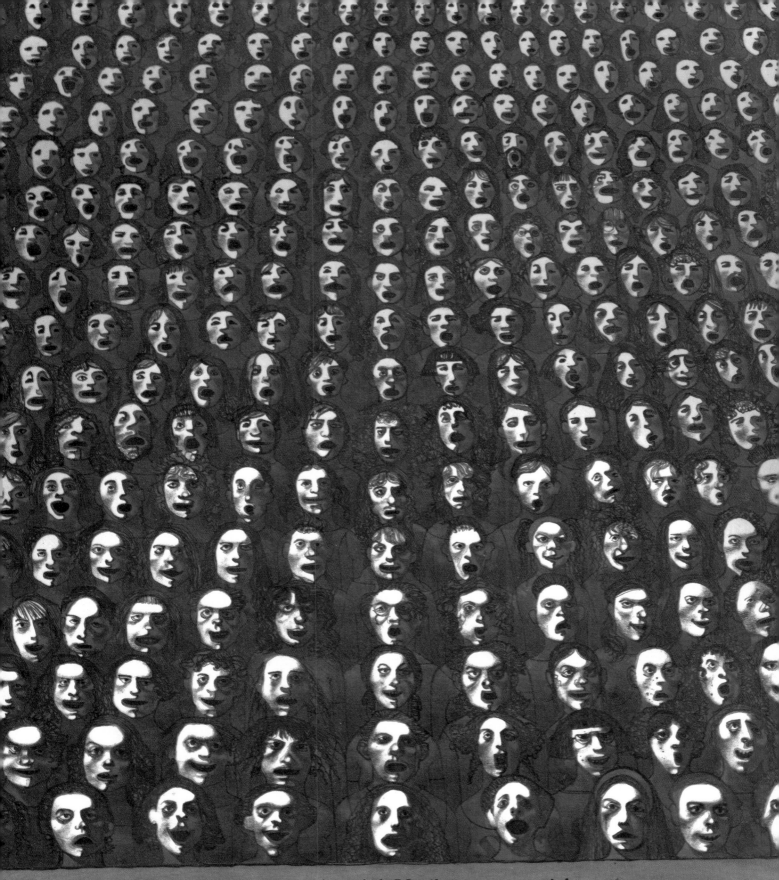

And scream and scream they did. Until some were sick.
The critic, Micky Raker of the *Daily Muck*, said Sammy was the
greatest ever – he had to write something, he'd had a boring day.

Sammy became a natural for television. True, the audience had gone, but he didn't notice in his desire to perform.

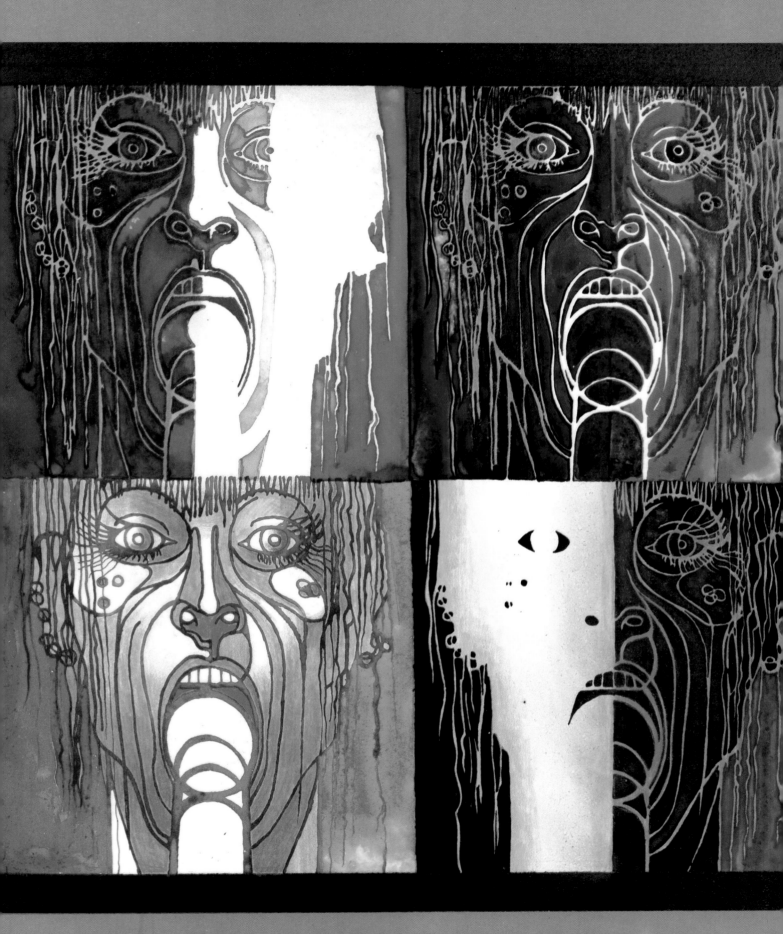

Mouthing to his own records, he mimed away in front of the camera, and they in turn flashed and fragmented his image in every home.

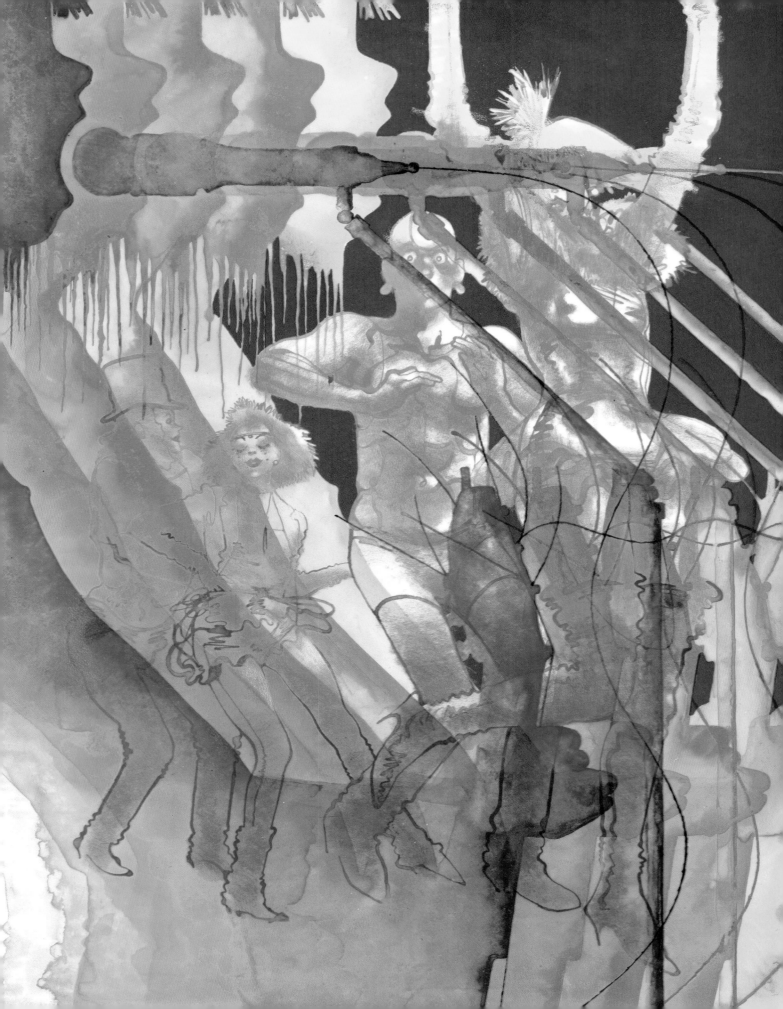

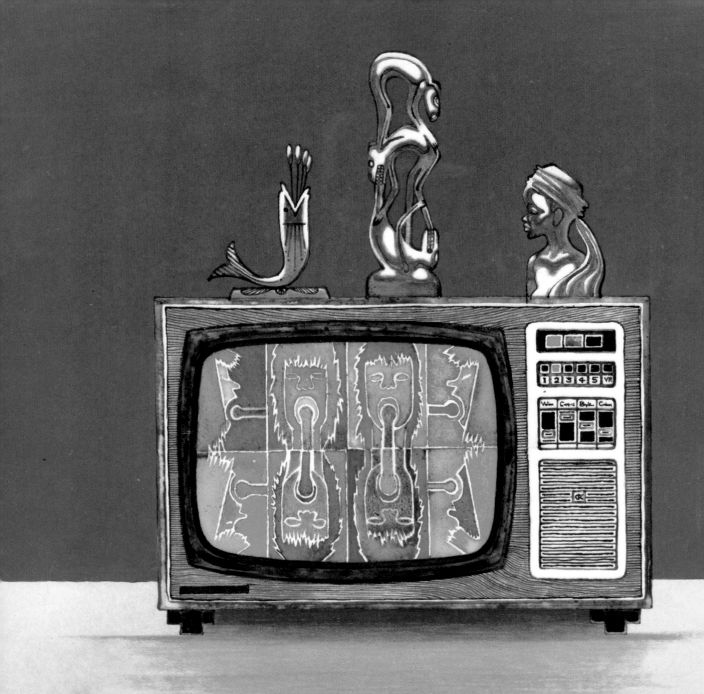

In time he really was only a small shape on the screen, lost in a barrage of coloured lights, loud noises, just a passing fragment with the news, advertisements, and chat shows.

Eventually, he was no more than a tiny video pack.

Sammy himself had moved into a great big house and lived in complete seclusion – a prisoner of his own fame. He stared out through the gates and saw no one. Even a dog didn't stop.

His videos became boring and were soon discarded and forgotten. In his weekly column Micky Raker called him 'a yesterday's man', 'a joke', and remarked that he was never anything more than a common streetsinger anyway.

A new face had come onto the scene – Syd Slicker and the Oil Slicks. Mjcky Raker had written glowing reviews about him, and it wasn't long before Mister Biggknob was bestowing his affections upon him, and treating him like a son.

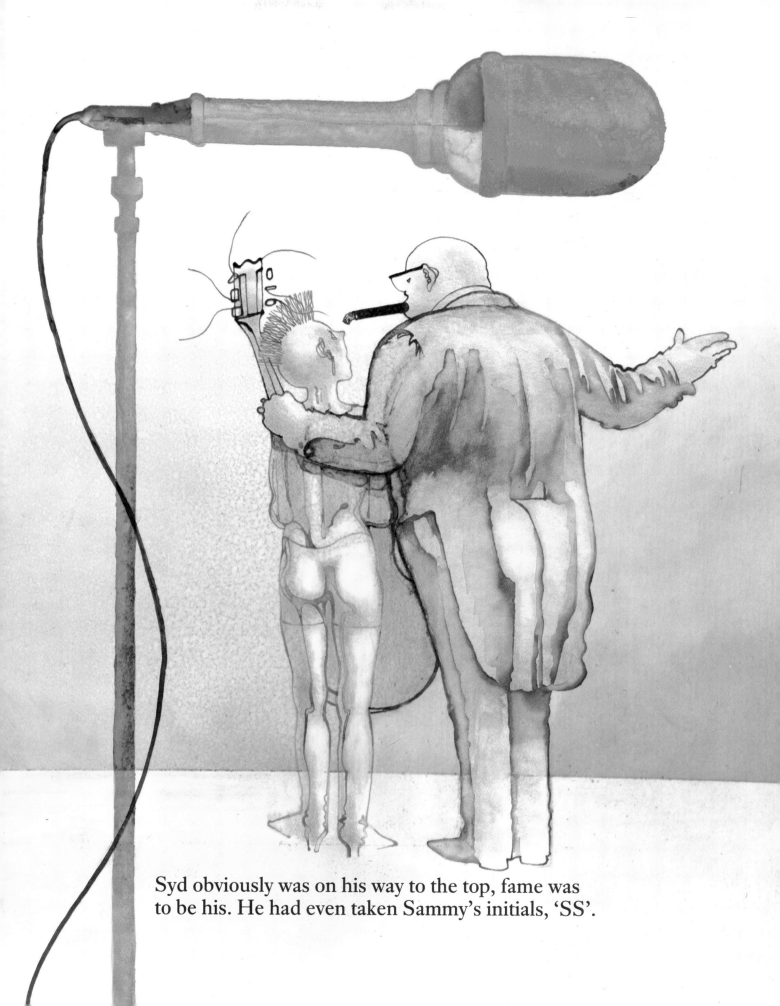

Syd obviously was on his way to the top, fame was
to be his. He had even taken Sammy's initials, 'SS'.

In an attempt to get back, Sammy sold his house and all his possessions and used the money to make a big spectacular film, a space epic.

But it was a flop. Only the poster was big and soon it was as forgotten as he was.

He was a nobody. Even the circus wouldn't have him back.

He sat in the park in the rain, feeling very sorry for himself.
Suddenly he became aware of two old friends watching him. In a
flash he knew what he must do. He still had his one-man band.

In no time he had changed his clothes and with his drum firmly in place on his back, he rushed through the streets and into the subway under the bypass.

Things hadn't changed much, and he felt secure and happy for the first time in a very long while.

So now he can be found, every day, with his old friends, bringing a little pleasure and gaiety into the lives of the people as they cross under the busy thoroughfare. A truly real entertainer. If you should see him, spare a coin and dance and sing with him.

LONDON'S EAST END DIESELS

By D. Brennand

ISBN 978-1-909625-57-0

ABBREVIATIONS USED THROUGHOUT THIS BOOK

BR	British Railways
BRCW	Birmingham Railway Carriage & Wagon Co.
BTH	British Thompson-Houston
DLR	Docklands Light Railway
DMU	Diesel Multiple Unit
DRS	Diesel Repair Shop
ECML	East Coast Main Line
ECR	Eastern Counties Railway
EE	English Electric Company
EMU	Electric Multiple Unit
ETH	Electric Train Heating
EWS	English Welsh & Scottish Railways
GER	Great Eastern Railway
GN	Great Northern
HST	High Speed Train
LEER	London's East End Railways
LNER	London North Eastern Railway
LNWR	London & North Western Railway
LT&SR	London Tilbury & Southend Railway
MET CAM	Metropolitan-Cammell
NB	North British Locomotive Company
NLR	North London Railway
NRM	National Railway Museum
PLA	Port of London Authority
RCTS	Railway Correspondence & Travel Society
SIFT	London (Stratford) International Freight Terminal
T&FGJR	Tottenham & Forest Gate Junction Railway
TOPS	Total Operations Processing System
WCML	West Coast Main Line

ACKNOWLEDGEMENTS

I would like to express my gratitude to the following people who have given me an enormous amount of help; Andy Meeks, Andy Grimmett, Arthur Nugent, Dave Cockle, Jim Connor, Peter Kay, Peter Manley, Murray Lewis, Grahame Wareham, Graham Weller, Andy Nash, Alan Williamson, Ken Wood, Graham Baker, Dave Underwood, Brian Pask, Geoff Silcock, Doug Fairhurst and of course, my long-suffering wife Belinda who meticulously proof reads all my diatribe. Also, the staff at Amadeus Press for their guidance and patience. If I have mistakenly missed anybody, it was not intentional.

Printed and bound by The Amadeus Press, Cleckheaton, West Yorkshire
First published in the United Kingdom by Book Law Publications, 382 Carlton Hill, Nottingham, NG4 1JA

INTRODUCTION

East London is a logical place to start looking back at the evolution of diesel locomotives. The country's first all diesel depot was sited at Devons Road (Bow) and the largest engine shed was just a couple of miles away at Stratford. The abolition of steam locomotives from the whole of East Anglia in September 1962 brought about a huge influx of diesels into this area over a relatively short period. Valuable and sometimes expensive lessons were quickly learned by British Railways with regard to the maintenance, reliability and suitability of the early pioneer diesel classes. Devons Road was very much a test bed for these new forms of traction with drivers, firemen and fitters raised in the steam age, quickly having to learn new skills. The Clean Air Act of 1956 and the British Railways Modernisation Plan of 1955 demanded cleaner forms of traction for the Nation's railways. London was heavily polluted at this time and huge numbers of steam hauled trains contributed to the problem. Only South London could boast a better air quality record due to the implementation of a widespread third rail electric system decades earlier. The East End had, of course, seen electric traction for suburban services between Liverpool Street and Shenfield since 1948, but much more was needed to improve people's health and offer better journey times.

By 1958 there was a drastic change, as several brand new diesel classes started to emerge from the English Electric, Brush, British Thompson-Houston and North British factories. The very first EE Type 1 Bo-Bo 1000 H. P. D8000 (now part of the National Collection) underwent trials in June 1957 and the first 20 were delivered to Devons Road shed (1D), thereby quickly ousting the smaller LMS 0-6-0 steam locos. The East London docks gave rise to a very large number of daily freight trains, with many originating from Poplar and Millwall; it was this area that witnessed the changing traction scene first hand, largely unseen by the travelling public, due to the closure of the Victoria Park to Poplar line to passenger trains in 1944. The cleaner, more clinical maintenance facilities required for diesel engines were problematic where old steam sheds were converted for the new traction. Devons Road would have been very costly if a brand new diesel shed had been provided, so the controlling Midland Region of BR decided to make do and mend by merely adding wooden raised platforms inside some of the shed roads, so that diesel fitters could access the side doors to the engine room of the new Type 1s. Prior to the closure of the North London Railway Bow Works in 1960, a small area of the old steam workshops was also used for diesel repairs.

We are still learning about the hazards and pollutants emitted by diesel engines, but back in 1958, most railway staff were pleased with the cleaner and warmer working environment provided by diesel traction. For men brought up in the tough world of steam engines, diesels must have seemed like the wonder of the age. The reality is that the diesel created a different type of pollution, which would last for several decades until more widespread use of electric traction evolved. The same region in control of Devons Road also had the responsibility of electrifying the West Coast Main Line just two or three years later with the provision of several brand new electric loco depots. This was one of the most interesting periods of our railway history, where steam, diesel and electric traction all worked alongside each other in unison. It was not uncommon for steam sheds to house diesel locomotives in the late 1950s, but the problem of cleanliness would not go away and much investment was urgently needed. The first diesel shed at Stratford in 1958 was a simple three road dead end affair, which then became the DMU shed after B&C sheds were opened in 1960. So many diesels arrived at Stratford in the late 1950s that the new facilities were overwhelmed, leading to some maintenance being carried out in the old Jubilee shed alongside hordes of steam engines. Even small particles of soot entering a diesel injector can cause havoc and the roof of a steam shed would have been heavily encrusted with years of soot being dislodged by the diesel and steam exhaust.

As steam came to an end at Stratford in the early 1960s, the depot underwent a radical and expensive rebuild. Half of the old 1887 Jubilee shed was demolished to make way for the new B & C shed, a vast 300 feet long by 80 feet wide building with a central office, mess room, stores and workshop area. With eight roads holding 16 main line locomotives, it was welcomed by all who worked on the diesels. It was clean, bright and had concrete raised platforms with pits beneath for easy access to all parts of the locomotives. Heavier repairs were sent to the Diesel Repair Shop, formerly known as the High Meads Repair Shop, which dated from the First World War. This building was converted for overhaul of diesels between 1958-9. By August 1960 the new B & C sheds were in use, but the grimy old Jubilee shed and its ghostly smoky inhabitants clung to its flank for three more years, reluctant to let go. It was finally demolished in 1963 along with the old coal tower, where explosive charges were attached to the legs. One loud explosion later, the tower crumbled and crashed to the ground ending a chapter of Stratford's illustrious history which had lasted almost 100 years. The depot would carry on for nearly four decades before finally succumbing to the inevitable but lamentable march of progress in 2001. English, Welsh & Scottish (EWS) railways opened a new £11m engine shed at the north end of Temple Mills yard in the same year, but this structure was very short lived. By 2007 it was demolished to make way for the Eurostar depot. The fascination of Stratford depot continues long after its demise. Many books and articles have been written, millions of photographs taken and probably several miles of cine film or video shot, but the appetite for more is seemingly endless. The depot, station and nearby marshalling yard at Temple Mills were fascinating places to while away the hours, either for pleasure or work. The diesel locomotives of our youth have largely disappeared, with just a handful of preserved examples from most classes left, enabling us to relive those far off carefree days. This volume is the last in the London's East End series (despite my assurance that I had no such plans at the end of Part 2) and I hope that it **serves as a lasting tribute to the diesel locomotive era.**

Note; the quality of certain pictures is not what you would expect, but these have been included on the grounds of rarity or in a few instances, uniqueness. The East End theme started out in good faith, and continues on from the previous two volumes. However, the boundaries have expanded into Essex, Middlesex and Hertfordshire. These were the hunting grounds of Stratford's fleet. Some beautiful pictures (especially those from Doug Fairhurst) came to light and needed to be shared, so apologies to the purists.

(*front cover*) **One diesel locomotive stands out when looking back at London's East End. The Brush Type (B) 2 A1A-A1A 1250 H.P. "Toffee Apple" No. D5500 was a pioneer, from what was to become a very successful locomotive class latterly known as the 31/0s. She entered service at Stratford in November 1957 and hauled her first passenger train (the 10.36 to Clacton) from Liverpool Street, surrounded by steam locomotives on all sides on 13th November. The "Toffee Apples", so called because of the shape of the drivers' controller handle, were always allocated to Stratford (30A) and therefore became synonymous with the East End traction scene for over 20 years. They first appeared with Mirrlees 12-cylinder engines, which proved troublesome and were replaced by more powerful English Electric 1470 H.P. engines in 1964. Upon withdrawal from BR in July 1976, D5500 was claimed for the National Collection and can be seen in beautifully restored condition at York. She is seen here on her home depot in 1969 alongside Brush Type 4 Co-Co 2750 H.P. No. D1799 which was only allocated to Stratford between May 1968 and January 1970. The NB alongside the loco number indicated that this 47 had no boiler fitted.** (*Author's Collection*)

(*back cover upper picture*) **Local historian and photographer Doug Fairhurst recorded much of the fast disappearing railway scene along the Lea Valley line in the 1960s. Many of his views have never been widely published and it is a great privilege to bring such wonderful scenes such as this to a wider audience. Class 16 North British Bo-Bo 800 H.P. No. D8407 works the Harlow Mill to Temple Mills empty limestone hoppers on 15th October 1967. The driver is a young Tony Robinson, who at the time of writing has been on the footplate over 50 years with millions of miles under his belt. What an achievement.** (*D. Fairhurst*)

(*back cover lower*) **We are looking towards Stratford in this view taken in May 1978 of shunting operations at Stratford Market goods yard. The main purpose of the yard was to unload fruit and vegetables in the long shed, but as this traffic declined, other types of freight were handled and the sidings were latterly used for storing the Overhead Line Wiring Trains that were formerly kept at Romford. Here we see 08269 shunting empty coal wagons from West Ham power station, whilst full wagons are waiting to be taken back to the power station. The large building to the right in the distance is the former Great Eastern Railway printing works.** (*P. Kay*)

(*opposite*) **The main reason that authors produce these books, is the desire to recreate some of the past and those formative years of our childhood. Personal recollections shared with so many others, is the only inspiration we need. It would be easy to sit back and enjoy these photos from the comfort of my settee, but that would be a selfish act and leave nothing for future generations to appreciate how our vast railway system evolved into what it is today. This view taken on 25th August 1966 has more personal memories than any other photo in this book. My route to and from school in the late 1960s took me underneath the LT&SR line at this point where the branch to Woodgrange Park diverges bottom left. The L shaped bend in the road is Barrington Road which passes underneath the tracks and heads off towards East Ham Car Sheds. Taking this route to school meant that I could idly sit by the line and enjoy the procession of freights going to and from Ripple Lane, often being late for lessons! Class 31/0 "Toffee Apple" Brush Type 2 A1A-A1A 1470 H.P. No. D5514 meanders off Barking flyover with a westbound mixed freight. The Underground District line is to the right and the Fenchurch Street to Shoeburyness line is on the far right. In the background is Howard's chemical factory which oozed some nasty smelling liquids into the passing River Roding.**

The sweeping curves of Devons road engine shed in its heyday are laid bare in this 1958 view taken from the coaling tower. A relatively new English Electric Type 1 Bo-Bo 1000 H.P. No. D8009 (20009) is perhaps rather embarrassingly being shunted by a Midland Fowler Class 4F 0-6-0. The diesels were not without their faults and there are many recorded cases of steam engines coming to the rescue of a failed diesel. LMS Jinty class 3F 0-6-0s and North London Railway 0-6-0s are dotted around the yard along with a Class 15 BTH 800 H.P. Bo-Bo poking its nose out of the shed. We are looking south and the old Spratts Dog Biscuit Factory dominates the skyline to the right as a freight passes on the busy Poplar line. *(Ken Wood Collection)*

A weekday scene at Devons Road with the majority of engines out on diagrams. In its heyday, in the LNWR period, the shed would have been a sight to behold. Here we see just one EE Type 1 Class 20 diesel accompanied by an LMS Jinty 3F 0-6-0 and an ancient North London Railway 0-6-0 3F No. 58857 first introduced in 1879, simmering on the right. *(Ken Wood Collection)*

Looking resplendent in its shiny new green colour scheme with a light grey roof, we see EE Type 1 Bo-Bo 1000 H.P. No. D8012 (20012) inside Devons Road shed. The simple wooden platforms added for fitters to access the engine bay bodyside doors are evident in the foreground. Fitters precariously teetered around on ladders to work on the locos, which was far from ideal or safe. Only two roads out of eight had these platforms. *(Ken Wood Collection)*

Ideally suited for the tight bends at Poplar and Millwall docks were these powerful North British design 0-4-0 diesel hydraulic 330 H.P. shunters. Only 14 were built and the first eight were delivered to Devons Road in 1958. The remainder went to Rugby, Nuneaton and Edge Hill. Here we see D2905/6 at Devons Road in 1961. By 1967 the whole class had been withdrawn and cut up. *(P. Paton/J. Connor Coll)*

British Thompson-Houston Type 1 Bo-Bo 800 H.P. No. D8202 stands outside Devons Road shed in the late 1950s. Even at such an early age, there is evidence of the engine oil leaks which plagued the class throughout their career. Other problems arose from coolant leaking into the cylinders causing piston failures. Hopefully, when the only survivor D8233 runs again, all the faults from the past will be eradicated. *(P. Paton/J. Connor Coll)*

Devons Road was surrounded on three sides by blocks of flats where the residents were serenaded by the sound of whistling Class 20s and Class 15s. Today, many enthusiasts would pay a handsome figure to wake up every morning to such delights! This 1958 view shows a relatively new EE Type 1 Bo-Bo 1000 H.P. No. D8005 (20005) resting quietly; perhaps the drivers were told to shut them down, so as not to cause a nuisance! *(P. Paton/J. Connor Coll)*

The air of neglect and dereliction that fell over the East End docks and the effect that the decline in rail traffic had in the mid-1960s is portrayed rather well in this view of Devons Road shed in the late 1960s. The North London Railway originally opened the shed in 1882. In just six years, this depot went from being the very first all diesel depot in 1958 to being completely abandoned by 1964. The site remained overgrown for decades before being claimed for housing. Docklands Light Railway services now run past the site. *(Authors Coll)*

A fascinating view of Millwall Junction in 1963 looking towards Fenchurch Street on what was the original route to Blackwall that had closed to passengers in 1926. The remains of the station could still be seen until the building of the DLR in the early 1980s. This vibrant freight scene is controlled by three signal boxes; Millwall Junction in the foreground, with Bank box just to the left and Poplar Loop Line box far right. BTH Type 1 No. D8201 overlooks West India Dock on the left and Harrow Lane sidings to the right. *(A. Powell)*

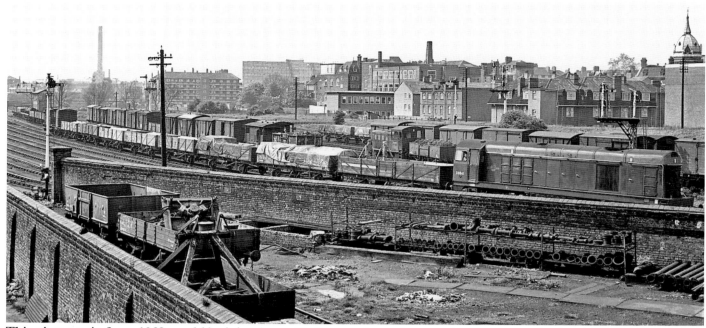

This view, again from 1963, could be joined up with the previous photo to give a panoramic view of Millwall Junction freight yards. This is Harrow Lane sidings and EE Type 1 Bo-Bo 1000 H.P. No. D8041 (20041) is about to leave with a northbound freight for the Midland Region. At this time there were two routes out of the Poplar complex; one via Salmons Lane curve on the Fenchurch Street line and the NLR route via Victoria Park. North British diesel shunter No. D2900 is mingling amongst the wagons. *(A. Powell)*

One of the Port of London Authority Yorkshire Engine Company 0-6-0 DE 300 H.P. locos comes off the PLA West India Dock exchange sidings in 1963. These locos arrived in 1959 to replace the aging steam fleet. They survived until the PLA abandoned all internal rail traffic in May 1970. This view is taken from the public footbridge which gave unparalleled views over the Millwall Junction site. The tracks seen here were once used by Millwall Junction to North Greenwich passenger trains, which ceased in 1926. *(A. Powell)*

Class 03 0-6-0 204 H.P. diesel shunter No. 03154 (D2154) rounds the curve from Harrow Lane sidings towards the site of the long-closed Poplar East India Dock Road station in 1979. We are looking north. The slow decline of Poplar East Dock was starting to be felt at this time with just two trains arriving and departing each weekday. Changing traffic patterns caused the final closure in the very early 1980s. *(G. Weller)*

Beyond Millwall Junction, the old London & Blackwall line continued in a cutting to Blackwall. The building of the power station on the station site in 1947 meant that the line was truncated before the terminus. This view shows the remains of the old Poplar (L&B) station on the 1st October 1960 during the visit of the RCTS "Northern Heights" railtour formed of a 6-car Metropolitan-Cammell DMU. The lines to the left are the Blackwall tracks heading off to a small scrap yard and the short branch to the right gives access to the old Great Northern goods depot. *(J.E. Connor Coll)*

A view from the overbridge looking north, showing Poplar Central signal box and the former Poplar East India Dock Road station, which had been closed since 1944. The docks area suffered many bombardments during WW2 and the stations, along with their passengers, were further victims of enemy action. This view is taken in 1962. (*J. S. Phillips*)

The snow covered platforms of the long closed Old Ford station on the Poplar branch are disturbed by a southbound freight to the docks on 28th January 1964. BTH Type 1 No. D8204 heads a delightful mix of wagons. The NLR station originally opened in 1867 and proved popular with the locals until WW2 when the whole line suffered from air attacks causing the premature demise of passenger trains. It closed officially on 23rd April 1945 but trains had ceased a year earlier. The ticket office remained open to sell tickets which were valid on replacement buses. The platform buildings were demolished in 1963 and the street level building soldiered on until 1967. (*J. Connor*)

An unidentified Brush Type 2 A1A-A1A 1470 H.P. loco in green with full yellow ends takes the Stratford line at Victoria Park junction in 1964 with a mixed freight train. The earth mound in the foreground is all that is left of the old Victoria Park station that closed on 8th November 1943, with the Poplar line stations quickly following. These lines were then mainly the domain of freight trains until a new Stratford Low Level to Camden Road service started in 1979, with new stations at Hackney Wick, Homerton and Hackney Central being added later. The box closed in October 1984. (*J. Connor Coll*)

Brush Type 2 No. D5511 (31011) passes through the long-closed Leman Street station between Fenchurch Street and Stepney in the late 1950s with an officers' special saloon. The loco is propelling the train and has an oil tail lamp. Of all the British Transport Commission designs of the 1950s, the "Toffee Apples" (D5500-D5519) were probably one of the greatest success stories, some lasting until 1980. *(P. Paton/J. Connor Coll)*

The Railway Correspondence & Travel Society (RCTS) organised the "The Great Eastern Suburban No. 2 Railtour" on 28th April 1962. For those lucky participants, there were some rare treats, some of which are impossible today. Using the N7 0-6-2T No. 69621 (which turned out to be the only preserved example) and one of only a handful of ancient 0-6-0 J15s left at Stratford, No. 65476, the tour took in Palace Gates, Chingford via Hall Farm Curve, Epping, Ongar and North Woolwich. The train is about to depart Liverpool Street and Brush Type 2 No. D5587 (31169) looks on enviously.

There was certainly an element of excitement and wonder when the brand new Class 40 English Electric Type 4 1 Co-Co1 2000 H.P. locomotives arrived on the Great Eastern in 1958 to replace the Britannia class steam locos on the Norwich services. Whether they lived up to the expectations is open to debate and they were not welcomed by some of the loco crews who found them underpowered. Undoubtedly, they were cleaner and warmer to work on in the winter but they had a job to do and that became a real challenge. D203 (40003) stands at the head of a Norwich service at Liverpool Street in 1960. *(M. Axcell)*

Liverpool Street in 1971 was largely unaltered from the Victorian era and had far more character than it has today. Here we see English Electric Type 3 Co-Co 1750 H.P. No. 6724 (37024) from March (31B) standing at the buffer stops on Platform 7. Passengers are just boarding the 14.36 express to Kings Lynn; with just 6 stops this was a good service. A variety of EMU classes populate the other West Side platforms. *(B. Brockbank)*

The magnificence of the West Side trainshed roof dwarfs the seemingly diminutive Class 08 shunting pilot in July 1976. There was little work for the pilot during the day, but at night there were numerous parcels and newspaper trains which needed remarshalling.

Class 37 no. 37054 (D6754) comes off Bethnal Green Junction with a Cambridge to Liverpool Street service on 2nd February 1980. Running alongside is a Class 306 EMU No. 085, originally built in 1948 and soon to be withdrawn due to new 315 units about to enter service at this time. The 306 units were very robust with excellent braking capabilities; the same cannot be said for their replacements, especially in slippery conditions! *(B. Daniels)*

Bethnal Green station has always had appeal to the enthusiast. Locos climbing up the gradient from Liverpool Street would often be working flat out, so whether that be steam or diesel, it has endured throughout the generations as a good vantage point. Even today, the odd trainspotter will be glimpsed here, although the forms of traction lack variety and diesels have virtually disappeared. Class 37 No. 37075 (D6775) rounds the curve with an Up express from Cambridge on 12th February 1980. *(B. Daniels)*

The carriage sidings at Thornton Fields were only ever glimpsed by the passing traveller, but this image from 4th August 1963 shows an English Electric Type 3 Co-Co 1750 H. P. diesel with very esteemed company in the shape of two Class 309 Clacton EMUs. Originally classified as class AM9, they entered service to much fanfare in 1962 and were immensely popular with the travelling public and train crews. With a top speed of 100 mph and good riding qualities from the Commonwealth bogies, they gave Clacton/Walton line customers greatly improved journey times. They stayed on the GE until January 1994 when some were transferred to Manchester. Here we see No's 602 and 607; two-car units with the pantograph on the cab roof, in attractive lined maroon livery.

Although it is well known that the first twenty English Electric Type 1 Bo-Bo 1000 H.P. locomotives started their career at Devons Road, photos of these straying onto Eastern Region territory are quite rare. This is D8012 (20012) carrying a 1D shedplate heading back to the Midland Region with a freight from Ripple Lane in 1960 as it passes through Stratford. The loco is sporting a typical hand crafted 'target' board which told signalmen and others which working the train was on. (M. Axcell)

Stratford Old Yard could be viewed from platform 13 on the Cambridge line. Class 08 0-6-0 350 H.P. No. D3499 stands by waiting for its next job in 1962. This loco was withdrawn in 1968. A classmate, yet to receive 'wasp stripes' is busy nearby; an indication of how much activity there was. This yard mainly dealt with passenger and parcels vehicles. The 08s were notoriously uncomfortable for loco crews, with nothing more than a tiny stool to sit on. *(D. Fairhurst)*

Although the quality is not very good, this is a rare view of BTH Type 1Bo-Bo 800 H. P. No. D8212 standing at TE 24 signal on the Loop line through Stratford depot in 1965. This is another one of those views often only obtainable by a railwayman. The train has come up from the docks via the Low Level and Fork Junction and waits for the road into Temple Mills yard. The driver is about to contact the signalman. *(J. Cole)*

The Hunslet Engine Company provided BR with just three of these diminutive 0-4-0 153 H.P. diesel shunters in 1955 for use in docks areas, such as Ipswich where tight curves were commonplace. Numbered D2950-D2952 (originally 11500–11502), they were fitted with cow-catchers and side skirts in their mid-careers. D2951 is seen at Stratford on 14th March 1958, probably undergoing such conversion work, seeing as the side rods and steps are missing. All three were withdrawn in 1967, with D2950 going into industrial use at Llanelli, but unfortunately, this was cut up in 1983.

(Booklaw Publications)

In what was most probably a posed publicity photo, new English Electric Type 4 1Co-Co1 2000 H.P. No. D200 (40122) stands alongside another newly built Brush Type 2 A1A-A1A 1250 H.P. No. D5500 (31018) in 1958. They stand outside the 3-road diesel shed at Stratford which later became the DMU shed. Alongside is a Derby Lightweight DMU Driving Trailer E79615. Stratford's Type 4s were quickly put to work on the Norwich services, ousting the Britannia steam locos. *(G.W. Sharpe)*

The year of 1958 certainly heralded a new era for diesel traction, with many untried classes of locomotive suddenly appearing from a variety of builders. The sad looking nose end of these North British (later Class 21/29) Bo-Bo Type 2 1100 H.P. machines was a portent of the sad lives they were to lead. Initially allocated to Stratford were No's D6110 – D6119 for use on the Great Eastern and Tilbury Southend lines. They were not a success and by 1960 they were sent packing back to Scotland, where they ironically had been built. This is a brand new D6114 outside the DRS on 7th June 1959 alongside another NBL product. *(Booklaw Publications)*

Prior to the electrification of the Lea Valley line between Cheshunt and Coppermill Junction, which was completed in March 1969, all the local services to Cheshunt and some services onto Hertford East, were in the hands of Class 125 Derby built, Rolls Royce powered DMUs. These were maintained at Stratford for their decade of service on the Lea Valley. This is power car E50993 alongside a Class 16 North British Type 1 and English Electric Type 4 No. D206 outside the DRS on 7th June 1959. *(Booklaw Publications)*

Robust and impressive English Electric Type 4 1Co-Co1 2000 H.P. No. D207, nestles beneath the equally imposing GER High Meads Locomotive Repair Shop on 7ᵗʰ June 1959. The building dated from the First World War, where its initial purpose was supplying munitions for the war effort. It was converted to deal with diesels in 1958, but the rudimentary ladders propped against the side of the loco indicate that there was still some time to go before fitters had proper platforms to access the bodyside and roof doors! *(Booklaw Publications)*

English Electric built two prototype 500 H.P. diesel shunting locos in 1956, numbered D226 and D227 (later D0226/ D0227). They carried one of the most unusual liveries around, at that time, but certainly not by today's standards! Being black with a bright orange bodyside stripe, they stood out amongst the more mundane liveries. Both were allocated to Stratford, where D0226 is seen outside the New Shed in September 1959. They were both withdrawn by 1960. This locomotive can now be seen on the Keighley & Worth Valley Railway in Yorkshire, whilst the other locomotive was scrapped.

(Booklaw Publications)

The early 1960s, saw just a handful of BR built Sulzer engined Type 2 Bo-Bo 1160 H.P. (later Class 24) locos allocated to Stratford. This example D5020 (24020) was allocated to Ipswich (32B) at this time. It is seen alongside Stratford's fuel point on 26th March 1961. The Eastern lost its allocation of these handsome machines by the mid-1960s, when they were concentrated on the Midland and Scottish Region's. This loco was withdrawn in 1975 and was cut up at Swindon two years later. *(Booklaw Publications)*

After being involved in a serious collision in 1967 with a BTH loco on Stratford shed, Brush Type 2 "Toffee Apple" No. D5518 (31101) was rebuilt with indicator boxes, blue star coupling code, and 90 mph gearing. Both cabs were severely damaged as seen here shortly after the collision. The cabs were so badly damaged that they had to be cut off. This was done at Stratford and might have contributed to the decision to convert the loco after the wiring looms were also cut through. After rebuilding at Doncaster it returned to service, but was no longer classified as Class 31/0. It survived into preservation and is currently located on the Battlefield Line at Shackerstone. *(J. Cole)*

Stratford once had several Class 04 Drewery 0-6-0 204 H.P. locos allocated to the depot for work in the smaller yards mainly around the docks. The first engines were introduced in 1952 and over the following nine years, over 140 were built. Here we see D2280 outside Stratford shed in 1967. Over 20 survive in preservation around the country. This loco was one of those fortunate examples; after being withdrawn in 1971 it went to Fords at Dagenham (No.2), eventually finding its way to the North Norfolk Railway. *(J. Searle)*

One of the best designed locomotives to appear in 1958 was the Class 15 BTH, but it had its drawbacks from the drivers' point of view; with the long nose running first, visibility was impaired on bends. Always at home on cross-London freights, the class were occasionally entrusted to work passenger trains in the summer months. They were never fitted with steam heating boilers. Here is D8225 on shed at Stratford in 1961. *(A. Grimmett Coll)*

The Class 03 204 H.P. diesel shunters were a familiar sight throughout East Anglia until the early 1980s with sizeable allocations at all the major sheds. This example, D2088, sits out of use minus its side rods, behind Stratford's New Shed in early 1973. It was a long-time Swindon (82C) engine but its final shed was Colchester (30E) from where it was withdrawn in July 1972. *(P. Manley)*

The iconic and familiar view of the depot in the diesel heyday of 1969 when there was still an element of variety. Class 15 BTH locos are still in abundance alongside the usual suspects in the shape of 31, 37, 47 and 08s. This view was taken from the old water tower. Legends handed down over the decades include stories of young secondmen and firemen swimming inside the water tank! *(J. Searle)*

The magnificent powerful lines of the English Electric Type 4 1Co-Co1 2000 H.P. machine are beautifully displayed in this view of D253 (40053) alongside the Diesel Repair Shop (DRS) in the early 1960s. This photograph was taken by the former Stratford driver and renowned photographer Jack Searle who loved railways and locomotives. Even after he retired, he still regularly visited the depot to sell his photos; sadly he is no longer with us. He was a true gentleman, a pleasure to know and leaves a wonderful legacy. *(J. Searle/N. Ottley Coll)*

Sitting idly and waiting patiently for its next turn we see Stratford (30A) allocated English Electric Type 3 Co-Co 1750 H.P. No. 6828 (37128) alongside B&C shed in the late 1960s. After the end of steam on BR in 1968 there was no need for the D prefix in front of diesel numbers, although a very large number still carried them until the TOPS renumbering scheme which started in 1972. Post 1972 these locos became Class 37s. *(J. Searle/N. Ottley Coll)*

Such frivolities as painting locomotives in special liveries is a practice that has just about disappeared from the main line network. Stratford selected Brush Type 4 Co-Co 2750 H.P. No. D1758 (47164) to receive such attention in the late 1960s and very fine it looks too, with a newly applied full yellow end and white wheel rims; note the 30A shedplate. This loco again carried a special livery in 1977 for the Queen's Silver Jubilee when it was chosen along with 47163 to carry a large Union Jack on each side. *(J. Searle/N. Ottley Coll)*

As Jack Searle is often mentioned in books about Stratford depot it seems only fair to include a picture of the man himself on what must have been one of the proudest days of his long railway career. He is seen on the right at Barking, meeting Her Majesty the Queen on the occasion of her visit to Stratford, Temple Mills and Barking on 15th February 1962. Jack was the driver of the Royal Train on this day and the booklet shown was his personal copy.

BRITISH TRANSPORT COMMISSION
BRITISH RAILWAYS

VISIT OF

HER MAJESTY QUEEN ELIZABETH II

TO THE

EASTERN REGION

THURSDAY, 15th FEBRUARY, 1962

PROGRAMME

Stratford's Brush Type 2 "Toffee Apple" No. D5508 (31008) has strange bedfellows in the shape of a pair of Class 24 'Baby Sulzer' Type 2 Bo-Bo 1160 H.P. diesels. These were a common sight in East London in the early 1960s with a sizeable allocation at Stratford, Ipswich and March. In the mid-1960s they were reallocated to the North-West and Scotland. *(Locophoto)*

Most weekdays during the 1970s and early 1980s, Stratford witnessed a daily visit from a Southern Region Class 33. This is Birmingham Railway Carriage & Wagon Co. Type 3 1550 H.P. No. 6592 (33207) waiting to leave Stratford International Freight Terminal (SIFT) with a freight in the early 1970s. This is one of the 12 so-called 'Slim Jim's' with a narrower body designed for working through the tunnels on the Tunbridge Wells – Hastings line. *(P. Manley)*

A delight for the happy spotter arriving at Stratford in the early 1970s at weekends would be row upon row of engines. Here we see a collection of Brush Type 2 "Toffee Apples" with 5515, 5510, 5501 and 5507 nearest the camera. This was taken in the relatively short period after the D prefix had been dropped and before TOPS numbering was introduced. It was not unusual to have over 70 locos on shed at weekends. *(P. Manley)*

Between 1972 and 1974, the old 'D' prefix loco numbering system was being phased out in favour of the TOPS numbering system, which was already widely used by the American Southern Pacific Railroad. Stratford's early attempts at renumbering are shown here on a Brush Type 2 'Toffee Apple', where just a small area of the bodyside has been repainted to cover the old D5502 number in favour of 31002, the new order. The loco is passing the original Great Eastern Railway locomotive works offices adjacent to Stratford Old Yard. *(P. Manley)*

The poor, unloved 1100 H. P. Bo-Bo Baby Deltics had a rather chequered career. From their launch in 1959 when all 10 were allocated to Hornsey (34B), they had several problems and by 1963 the whole fleet was out of action and stored at Stratford. Even after expensive rebuilds, they were non-standard and had all been withdrawn by 1971. These two lingered at Stratford after withdrawal for two years; D5909 being the only one to receive BR blue livery. The other example is D5905. *(P. Manley)*

Brush Type 2 A1A-A1A 1470 H.P. No. D5574 (31156) passes the wonderfully industrial backdrop of Angel Road Gas Works with an Up road express on 6th May 1963. The station is just behind the rear of the train. The gas works supplied a large area of North London and ceased operation in 1972.

No apologies for yet another view of Angel Road Gas Works. The dark foreboding structure dominating the scene is just as interesting, if not more interesting, than a train passing through a beautifully manicured pasture at Shap Summit (for me, anyway!). English Electric Type 3 Co-Co 1750 H.P, No. D6724 (37024) provides the motive power for this Down road Cambridge express on 6th May 1963. A motley collection of wooden and steel bodied coal wagons wait to disgorge their load into the ovens.

Palace Gates was very much an outpost of the Great Eastern system, built to rival the Great Northern Railway's service at Wood Green, serving Alexandra Palace. Passengers alighting here, had to walk over half a mile to the palace however. Once the service between North Woolwich and Palace Gates lost steam traction in 1961, the Class 31s took over briefly until closure of the branch to passengers on 7th January 1963. Having run round its train, D5659 (31232) is ready to depart for North Woolwich on 13th October 1962. Note the abundance of BR dark blue enamel signs; now very collectable. *(D. Dalton)*

Another view of Brush Type 2 No. D5659 at a seemingly deserted Palace Gates on 11th October 1962. Passenger numbers on the branch from Seven Sisters were very low at this time and it came as no surprise when the branch closed a few months later. Ticket receipts would have barely covered the running costs and staff wages. The rather quaint station was hidden in the back streets of Wood Green, largely unnoticed by the travelling public. *(D. Dalton)*

A view of Stratford Low Level in 1970 taken from Stratford Southern signal box. The formation of the Eastern Curve can be made out to the right of the Engineers' offices on the right. The large building on the left is the Engineers' workshop. A Class 104 Gloucester Railway Carriage & Wagon Company DMU has arrived with a service from North Woolwich. *(P. Manley)*

During 1955 the London Tilbury Southend line was chosen to conduct trials of the unique North British Bo Bo 827 H.P. diesel locomotive No. 10800. Designed by Ivatt during LMS days, it finally appeared in 1950, by which time BR had taken over. The locomotive could be considered as a prototype for the later Class 15 and 16s, which shared the same basic design. It is seen here on a test train at Barking East Junction on 3rd February 1955. The Underground lines to Upminster can be seen on the left. *(BR/Authors Collection)*

Taken from the cab of an 08 diesel shunter we see the miniature signal pulled off by the Abbey Mills Junction signalman for the train to enter the goods lines. We are looking north towards Stratford in April 1974. The loco is working empty wagons back to Temple Mills from Silvertown yard. The bridge in the distance carries the LT&SR line and there was a connection to this line via an incline, but this had been severed several years previously. *(P. Manley)*

Brush Type 2 A1A-A1A 1470 H.P. No. D5659 is seen again at North Woolwich on 11th October 1962. The old LNER stock and the run-down docklands were a perfect combination combined with the novelty of diesel hauled suburban services. The snake-like route taken to Palace Gates would take in panoramic views of Stratford depot and Temple Mills marshalling yard before reaching the junctions at Tottenham and Seven Sisters. *(D. Dalton)*

The unusual sight of a 6-car Cravens Class 105 DMU at North Woolwich whilst working an RTS Railtour in the early 1970s. The class were a common sight on this line. Built between 1956 and 1959, they served BR well, but all were withdrawn by 1988. They did not fare well when it came to preservation due to the presence of asbestos. Only three cars have been preserved. *(www.britishrailwayphotographs.com)*

This view of Class 47 No. 1608 (47478) is taken in the west reception yard at Ripple Lane in the early 1970s. This was a Llandore (Swansea) allocated engine at this time. The 47 is about to work the train through to Thames Haven oil refinery on the Thames estuary. Ripple Lane was a difficult place to reach, being a long walk from Dagenham Dock station. I often cycled there as a kid from Manor Park to witness the variety of engines and freight.

English Electric Type 3 Co-Co 1750 H.P. No. D6767 (37067) heads west over Barking Flyover in 1964 with a train of brand new Ford Cortina's and Zephyr's from Dagenham. The flyover gave passengers and freight customers' huge time saving benefits. The previous junction on level ground caused a lot of delays. The clever flyover design and that of the track layout incorporating the Underground lines (seen under the flyover) must have bought about a sigh of relief upon its completion.
(BR/Authors Coll)

A rare view of a green Class 40 with full yellow ends at Ripple Lane in 1970. D353 (40153) was a 52A Gateshead (Newcastle) engine at this time. She appears to have suffered a serious rather unsightly oil leak, which might explain the visit to the depot. Inter-regional freight was the mainstay of the North Thameside area and you never knew what sort of surprises would arrive at the head of the next train. *(Martyn Mugridge)*

We often forget the human aspect of railways. The crews of locomotives have immense knowledge, whether it is the inner workings of an engine, the intricate junctions and signalling layouts or the complexities of the rule book. They are the unsung heroes of our railways, getting in and out of bed at the most unsociable times imaginable and working long and sometimes lonely hours. On the plus side, the thrill of driving a diesel loco at speed with a heavy train outweighs all the negative aspects. Our driver climbs up into the cab of Brush Type 4 Co-Co 2750 H. P. No. D1608 (47478) as he prepares the loco for its day's work at Ripple Lane in the early 1970s.

The old and the new meet at Liverpool Street in 1960. Brush Type 2 No. D5530 (31112) is just a few months old and has a remarkably clean roof. The soon to be replaced N7 0-6-2T No. 69696 sits in the engine dock between platforms 12 and 13. In the background are several Class 306 and 307 EMUs in all over green livery. *(Author's Coll)*

Please do not adjust your set! This rather garish experimental colour scheme was applied to Brush Type 2 No. D5579 (31161) in 1961 and lasted for several years. D5578 also carried an experimental shade of blue long before BR blue was dreamt up. This colour was officially known as golden ochre. The only other loco to carry this livery in the 1960s was Class 52 diesel hydraulic D1015 "Western Champion" which is now preserved. D5579 is seen at Liverpool Street in March 1961. *(G. Wareham)*

Class 15 BTH B0-Bo 800 H.P. No. D8236 waits to depart Liverpool Street on 6th October 1962 with the Railway Correspondence & Travel Society "East London No. 3 Railtour". A very interesting itinerary included the North Woolwich line with deviations to Beckton and the Silvertown Tramway. Further afield, the train also visited Buntingford and the Southbury Loop which was newly electrified. *(Unknown/Authors Coll)*

This was the true heyday of London's East End diesels; steam had just been banished from the whole network, although East Anglia had lost steam, some six years previously. This is Liverpool Street with Brush Type 4 Co-Co 2750 H.P. No. D1527 of Stratford (note the painted shed code) idling away at the head of 1N20 to Norwich in 1968. In the background is a Type 1 BTH Class 15 Bo-Bo 800 H.P. loco on station pilot duties; most probably D8234 which was a regular loco on this turn. *(Authors Coll)*

Unusually for a Stratford based locomotive, Brush Type 4 Co-Co 2750 H.P. No. D1792 (47311) carries patched up green paintwork in this August 1969 view at Liverpool Street. The lighter Sherwood Green has also had some less noticeable touch-in work. This illustrates perfectly how the chemicals in washer plants caused paintwork to fade. The loco is at the head of a Norwich service in platform nine. *(G. Wareham)*

Another example of a literally half-baked paint job on another Brush Type 4, No. D1771 (47176) in the loco sidings at Liverpool Street with two other classmates in April 1970. The left hand end of the lighter Sherwood Green has been repainted and the right hand end is still original. There is a prototype for everything it seems. *(G. Wareham)*

English Electric Type 3 Co-Co 1750 H.P. No. D6754 rests after arriving at Liverpool Street platform 12 with an Up road express on 31st May 1970. The rather tired looking original green paintwork would soon be covered in good old BR blue and the TOPS number 37054 – I know what livery I prefer, but that shows my age! *(Author's Coll)*

The loco fuel point at Liverpool Street was busy all day with loco hauled services to Cambridge, Kings Lynn, Harwich, Norwich and the occasional Lowestoft; the thirsty engines needed replenishing and Class 37 No. 37047 (D6747) stands by for its next turn on 8th August 1978. The building on the left housed the yard shunter, fuellers and fitters. The old four character headcode system is being phased out and replaced by two white dots, making it very difficult to know which train a loco is working when researching for books! *(B. Daniels)*

The last of the Toffee Apple Class 31s, No. 31019 (D5519) is about to depart from Liverpool Street with an empty stock train for Thornton Fields carriage sidings on 31st August 1980. This loco was withdrawn from service just two months later along with the other remaining members of the class. Class 47 No. 47085 (D1670) "Mammoth" sits in the loco sidings. This was one of the original WR named 47s, which was named in 1965. The nameplates went missing in 1975 and again in 1984. On both occasions they were replaced, so there could be six "Mammoth" nameplates which have all been carried! *(Author's Coll)*

A reminder of locomotive hauled passenger trains on the Liverpool Street to Cambridge line on 9th October 1979, as Class 37 Type 3 Co-Co 1750 H.P. No. 37049 waits patiently at the signal on platform seven, before going into the loco sidings for refuelling. The engine is beautifully framed by the trainshed roof, which has survived the rebuilding and can still be enjoyed today. *(Author's Coll)*

Class 31 A1A-A1A 1470 H.P. No. 31418 (D5522) backs onto its train at Liverpool Street in 1979. The loco is unusual in having no roof indicator box (Skinhead), but being converted for Electric Train Heating (ETH). By this time, the old indicator discs were no longer being used to denote the train's headcode, but two of the original four have been retained in the old Class 1 passenger configuration. *(Author's Collection)*

Class 47 No. 47117 (D1705) of Stratford depot is getting impatient to work the next Norwich bound service in the early 1980s. Alongside is Class 37 No. 37110 (D6810) from March (31B) simmering before taking charge of a Cambridge train. The 47 and the station pilot are in platform 10 dock. Liverpool Street station is still resplendent in all its Victorian glory, before being butchered at the end of the decade. *(Author's Coll)*

If you wanted to capture a picture of an immaculate Class 08 0-6-0 350 H.P. diesel shunter, you would rarely be disappointed by the Liverpool Street pilot, as seen here in 1981. Beyond 08527 (D3689) is the murky depths of platform 10 Dock which was one of the less salubrious parts of the station. The sight and sound of a working 08 has all but disappeared from East London, with just two left at Ilford Car Sheds. *(Author's Coll)*

From the heyday of locomotive hauled trains to Cambridge, we see Class 37 Co-Co 1750 H.P. No. 37087 (D6787) sitting in 10 Dock adjacent to Platform 10 at Liverpool Street in the early 1980s. This was a March and Stratford engine between 1976 until 1989. Alongside is the once familiar tank wagon full of diesel fuel to replenish the underground tanks at the fuelling point. Several of these tank wagons were emptied every week by the thirsty diesel fleet. *(Authors Coll)*

The unusual sight of the test coach Mentor arriving at Platform 10 Liverpool Street in May 1981 behind Class 47 No. 47314. This coach was being used to monitor the overhead line equipment; a job which it still does for Network Rail at the time of writing. The locomotive was allocated to Immingham (40B) freight depot and would have been a rare 'cop' for any trainspotters at Liverpool Street. *(Authors Coll)*

Brush Type 2 No. D5654 (31228) stands at the head of a Great Northern service at Broad Street station in 1968; the final year of loco hauled services before going over to DMUs from 5th May 1969. No less than eight loco hauled trains for Gordon Hill, Hertford North, Cuffley and Potters Bar, left in the afternoon peak between 17.05 and 18.35. Third rail Class 501 electric units worked the Richmond services until the closure of the station in 1986. Before the Second World War, services to Poplar originated from here and would use the former Eastern curve at Dalston Junction. *(J. Connor)*

A very rare visitor in the shape of a Class 127 1959 Derby built 4-car DMU, normally seen only on the St. Pancras to Bedford line, passes through the closed NLR Shoreditch station in 1966. The delightfully rustic and weathered platform buildings are captured just before they were finally demolished. Those on the island platform were swept away the previous year; remarkable survivors considering that the station was closed in 1940. The railcar is heading away from Broad Street. *(J. E. Connor)*

English Electric Type 2 Bo-Bo 1100 H.P. 'Baby Deltic' No. D5902 passes through Dalston Junction station at speed on its way from Finsbury Park depot to Broad Street in March 1969, just 2 months before diesel hauled services ended. These are probably the only design from English Electric that can be considered a failure. When introduced in 1959, the front ends had disc indicators, gangway doors and ladders on the nose ends. The whole class had new noses and modified engines fitted in the mid-60s. *(G. Wareham)*

Although steam traction was still very much the dominant force at Devons Road shed in late 1957 when this view was taken, it has been cleverly removed from the scene to portray the 'New Diesel Dawn'. Brand new English Electric Type 1 Bo-Bo 1000 H.P. D8000 (the first of the class) would have been the centre of attention from drivers, firemen and fitters, all keen to get their hands on their new toy! This locomotive was renumbered 20050 in the early 1970s and is now part of the National Collection. *(A. Nugent)*

Although not of the best quality, this is the only view I'm aware of showing a Class 20 with half yellow ends at Devons Road shed in 1963. The loco is D8040 (20040), which was allocated to Devons Road at this time. An all green classmate peers out of the shed. Due to the severe decline in freight traffic from Poplar in the mid-1960s, Devons Road closed in the following year. All the locos, drivers and fitters were moved to either Stratford or Willesden depots. *(Unknown/Authors Coll)*

The site of Devons Road (1D) engine shed in the heart of Bow remained derelict for many years before being totally cleared for redevelopment. This is the rather dilapidated state of the building as it was in 1975 after half of the structure had been demolished. Compare this to the earlier views to see how many details remain on the structure. Lamps, ladders, doors and roof vents are all intact. We are looking south towards Poplar. *(M. Lewis)*

Good quality colour views of diesels working in and around Poplar are surprisingly rare. It would be wonderful to find views of Class 20s or 15s in this area, but all my efforts have come up with nothing except this. They will no doubt surface after publication, as has happened in the past. Here we see Class 03 0-6-0 204 H. P. No. 03047 (D2047) shunting Harrow Lane sidings at Poplar circa 1980. The building on the left is the old NLR goods offices and in the background is the site of Poplar East India Dock Road station. *(C. Stephens)*

Pure nostalgia, as Class 08 0-6-0 350 H.P. shunter No. D3300 (08230) pulls Cravens power car No. E51292 out of Stratford Old Yard in 1964. This is a good old days, pre Health & Safety picture with the shunter himself riding on the back of the DMU – love it! Platform 13 on the Cambridge line is behind and the original GER loco works offices can just be glimpsed to the far left. *(Author's Coll)*

A busy scene at Stratford on a sunny day in 1969. The local motive power is out in force, with a pair of Brush Type 2s in multiple running light engine towards the loco depot and a BTH Type 1 No. D8221 heading towards Temple Mills with a freight. The 31s are both in green livery with their distinctive white bodyside stripes. Platforms 11 and 12 still have their GER canopies. *(Author's Coll.)*

Early colour pictures of Class 20s working on the Stratford to North Woolwich line are rare. Here we witness a Devons Road (1D) EE Type 1 Bo-Bo 1000 H.P. loco passing Stratford Low Level with a freight from the docks in 1960. The loco carries one of the Devons Road 'target' numbers on the front which denoted which engine diagram the loco was on. Two delightful bracket signals and Stratford Southern box on stilts overlook the scene. *(Author's Coll)*

Cravens Class 105 DMU calls at a somewhat run-down Canning Town in 1978 with a Stratford Low Level to North Woolwich service. The survival of GER benches and LNER cast iron names on them is notable. The station once had substantial platform buildings and canopies. To the right is the old LNWR goods yard which is being used by a scrap dealer. The cooling towers belong to West Ham Power Station. *(P. Kay)*

From 1st May 1970, the Port of London Authority ceased all rail born freight around the Royal Docks. This was a terrific blow to the East End economy and local jobs. This rather sad view was taken just two days after the cessation of traffic at the Custom House PLA Exchange sidings, with rusty rails already taking hold. Within a short time, all the wagons would be removed and the engines would return to their nearby shed to await resale or scrap. Custom House station is just in view on the right. *(Author's Coll)*

The very unusual sight of Class 08 350 H.P. 0-6-0 diesel shunter No. D4192 (08958) on a brake van tour of the docks on 30th March 1963. The tour was organised by the RCTS due to the failure of a previous tour on 6th October 1962 to traverse the Silvertown Tramway (a photo of this train appears on Page 74 L.E.E.R. Part 2). The brake van tour was hauled by the 08 from Stratford Low Level to North Woolwich (seen here), then along the Silvertown Tramway, back to Thames Wharf Junction, then over the truncated portion of the Tramway's western spur. *(B. Pask)*

This is a very rare occurrence, as Birmingham Railway Carriage & Wagon Co. (later Class 27) Bo-Bo 1250 H.P. No. D5408 (27115/27209) of Cricklewood (14A) pauses briefly whilst working a freight from the docks back to the Midland Region in 1965. It has just passed through Stratford Low Level, turning right at Fork Junction and entering the old Stratford Loop Line running through the depot. The Midland men would probably have had a pilot driver for this working, and he may be the man on the left. *(Author's Coll)*

During 1967 the Class 40 English Electric 2000 H.P. Type 4s were replaced by more powerful Class 47s on the Norwich main line. Here we see Brush Type 4 Co-Co 2750 H.P. No. D1770 at the head of an Up express passing through Stratford in 1968. Alongside is the once familiar sight of a Class 306 EMU on a Liverpool Street to Shenfield working. *(Author's Coll)*

A panoramic view of Stratford and Channelsea sidings in the very early 1970s looking east. The view today would be from the Olympic swimming pool and would not be so rewarding. Here we see a Class 37 hauling a train of Cartic carriers containing brand new Ford Cortina's from Dagenham. The sidings hold a wonderful variety of rolling stock and in the foreground is the former Carpenters Road goods depot. *(H. E. Jones)*

Stratford station in the 1970s was a haven for trainspotters looking out for unusual workings from other regions. Taken on 1st September 1970 we see a Class 101 Metropolitan-Cammell 3-car DMU on its way for attention at the Diesel Repair Shop. This may have come from Cambridge, Norwich or even Leeds. Two independent sources witnessed Blue Pullman units passing through Stratford going to the works in the early 70s – what a shame that photos can't be found. *(Author's Coll)*

Class 31 Brush A1A-A1A 1470 H. P. No. 31125 (D5543) comes off Channelsea curve with an eastbound freight. A mid-1970s view when East London still had several functioning goods yards at Bow Midland, Manor Park, Romford and Upton Park. This is likely to be the Upton Park working with a brake van each end for running round at Barking. *(Author's Coll)*

Class 31 No. 31114 (D5532) glides through Stratford with a delightful rake of empty 6-wheeled milk tanks from the milk depot at Ilford on 21st July 1979. The handsome chap in the seat is Stratford driver Herbie White, who I had the pleasure of working with on several occasions. Despite the grimy external condition of the tanks (one still carries St. Ivel red and white livery), the insides were glass lined and were thoroughly cleaned daily. We worked these to Channelsea sidings, Kensington Olympia or Acton. By 1981 the milk traffic had ceased. *(B. Daniels)*

A 1983 view of English Electric Type 3 Co-Co 1750 H.P. No. 37102 (D6802) thundering through Stratford with a Liverpool Street to Harwich Parkeston Quay Boat Train. You can almost feel the ground shake as 102 tons of locomotive roars over the pointwork. *(M. Lewis)*

Stratford's allocation of Class 105 Cravens DMUs were often pressed into service at weekends, when they were not required for the North Woolwich line service. Here we see a 6-car formation running into platform eight at Stratford on a Southend Victoria bound service in the mid-1980s when the overhead power had been switched off for engineering work. The diesel units would have really struggled to keep up with the electric timings. *(Author's Coll)*

Double-heading of Freightliner trains was a common sight in the mid-80s. The challenge of powering over 1200 tons up Brentwood bank for a single 37 would be too much. This is 37168 (D6868) and another classmate coming off Channelsea curve with an eastbound working. *(Author's Coll)*

One of the Southern Region's quirky Electro-Diesels heads towards the North London line propelling an Inspection Saloon being used for driver route training on 22nd October 1985. These were an uncommon sight at Stratford. Originally built in 1962, they were later classified as Class 73. They ran off the third rail system but also had the luxury of a 600 H. P. diesel engine which is in use here. This is No. 73006 (E6006) of Stewarts Lane depot (75D). *(Author's Coll)*

A down road Liverpool Street Norwich express is powered by Class 47 Brush Type 4 Co-Co 2750 H.P. No 47429 (D1541) on 13th July 1983 with a train of Mark 2 stock in tow. It has been a long tradition that the Great Eastern section of BR got cast offs from other regions when it came to motive power and rolling stock. However, it was an improvement as the coaches had electric train heating replacing the old steam heating. *(M. Lewis)*

Class 47 No. 47008 (D1530) passes through platform nine with a Cartic train from Dagenham on 13th July 1983. Ford Sierra's and Fiesta's form the bulk of the load or 'Dagenham Dustbins' as we used to call them (affectionately, of course!). A relatively new Class 315 EMU is leaving platform eight – these are still running, some 35 years after being introduced. *(M. Lewis)*

The Class 56 heavy freight locomotives were first introduced in 1976, with the first 30 being built in Romania. They were equipped with 3250 H.P. Ruston Paxman engines. The leading locomotive in this view is 56031 "Merehead" (the first of the Doncaster built locos), double-headed with 56034, working the Purfleet to Merehead stone empties on 12th July 1984 passing Stratford. Several are still in service and five have been preserved. *(A. Nugent)*

British Rail built Class 58 Type 5 Co-Co 3300 H.P. No. 58034 "Bassetlaw" rounds the curve at Channelsea after negotiating the junction at Stratford with a failed Class 47, No. 47473 and a Cartic train on 16th March 1999. First introduced in 1983, they had the same power as a Deltic, but were purely designed for freight use and had a top speed of 80 mph. After just 20 years in service, they were usurped by the influx of Class 66 locos in huge numbers. This loco is currently stored in France! *(A. Grimmett)*

Somewhere along the line, locomotive designs have become far more angular. Gone are the days of smooth curves produced by the English Electric factory. The Type 5 Co-Co 3100 H.P. Class 60s came onto the scene in 1989 and 100 were eventually built by Brush at Loughborough. There are much less than half the class still in service and they are rarely seen in East London today. Here we see No. 60073 "Cairn Gorm" in Bow Midland yard in 2000. The old Bryant & May match factory, now converted into flats, overlooks the scene. *(A. Grimmett)*

The earliest diesels at Stratford were the Drewery class shunters introduced from 1955 when numbers 11121-11135 (later D2215-D2229) arrived. These were joined by the handsome Derby Lightweight diesel multiple units in the same year. These were hugely successful and popular units which quickly ousted steam on many rural branch lines. This example is seen at Stratford in 1958. In the background is one of Stratford's old GER Y4 0-4-0T steam locos, probably No. 33 (68129), used for depot shunting. *(Authors Coll)*

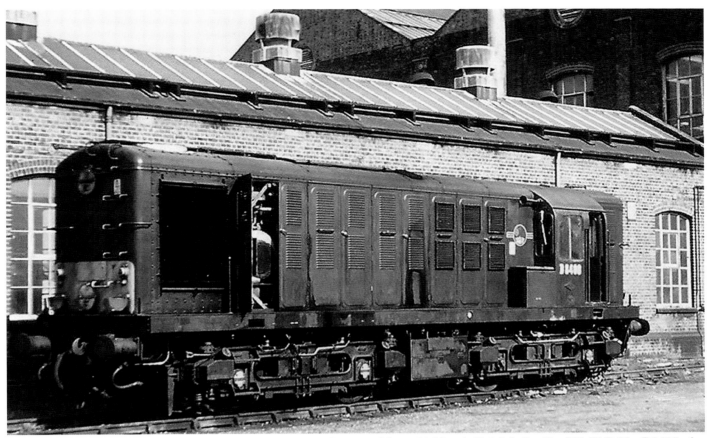

With its trademark oil leaks more than evident, a forlorn Class 16 North British Bo-Bo 800 H.P. No D8408 sits outside the back of the Diesel Repair shop in 1967. Many of these locos spent more time under repair than they did in traffic. They were occasionally entrusted to work passenger trains. Understandably, the whole class was withdrawn the following year. *(J. Connor)*

Brush Type 2 A1A-A1A 1470 H.P. "Toffee Apple" No. D5509 rests at Stratford in November 1967. The livery carried here, although nicely work-stained, really suited the locos, and the application of BR blue over the following years was the unacceptable march of progress. The red dots above the buffers made the Toffee Apple's non-standard when coupled in multiple. They could only be coupled to other red dot (electro-magnetic) fitted classes. All other 31s had the more widely used blue star (electro-pneumatic) multiple control system. *(G. Wareham)*

Arguably the best livery ever carried by the Class 37s was BR green with a grey roof and half yellow warning panels. This is EE Type 3 Co-Co 1750 H.P. No. D6723 (37023) by Stratford's giant steam era water tower in the late 1960s. *(Unknown/ Author's Coll)*

Withdrawn Class 16 NBL Bo-Bo 800 H.P. No. D8407 and another classmate sit by Stratford's fuel point in April 1969. Ironically, it would never be fuelled again as the whole class of 10 locos (always Stratford engines) had been withdrawn the previous year. Only a few ever received full yellow ends and none were ever repainted BR blue. This example was cut up at Kettering the following December. *(Author's Coll)*

Class 04 Drewery 0-6-0 204 H.P. No. D2215 spent its whole career at Stratford. It was introduced in July 1955 in black livery as 11121 and became D2215 in March 1960. It is seen here shortly after withdrawal in 1969. In equally work-stained condition is Class 08 0-6-0 350 H.P. No. D3629, which was a long-time (Peterborough) New England (34E) loco, withdrawn in 1968. *(G.W. Sharpe coll)*

Pioneer Class 15 BTH Type 1 Bo-Bo 800 H.P. No. D8200 was a long-time East End sight. Initially allocated to Devons Road (1D) in 1958, it was reallocated to Stratford in the mid-1960s after a brief spell at Norwich (32A). When first built, the loco was tested in brown undercoat over the Settle & Carlisle route in October 1957. It is seen here at Stratford alongside Class 31 No. D5525 in the late 1960s. The loco should have surely been a candidate for the National Collection, but was scrapped at Crewe in 1972. *(J. Connor)*

A fine portrait of Brush Type 4 Co-Co 2750 H.P. No. 1777 (47182) outside Stratford C shed in April 1970. Undoubtedly one of the greatest BR traction success stories, with 512 built and 508 in service at this time, they truly became the Jack of all Trades and reached every corner of the country. Four were withdrawn quite early due to serious accident damage. Over 80 still exist, with around 30 preserved. *(G. Wareham)*

Standing outside Stratford's Diesel Repair Shop in April 1970 is Class 23 Baby Deltic Bo-Bo 1100 H.P. No. D5902; often seen on local services out of Kings Cross until 1971 when the whole class of just 10 locos was withdrawn. The fitters at Stratford and Finsbury Park must have been relieved, as they were troublesome beasts; handsome nevertheless. *(G. Wareham)*

A decision by the Port of London Authority to end all rail born internal traffic from the Royal Docks in 1970 had quite a knock on effect with regard to Stratford's motive power requirements. Between March 1968 and March 1971 the whole class of BTH Class 15 diesels was withdrawn from service – all 44 of them. Some of the decline was due to containerisation; the class being unsuitable for such work. Here we see some of the redundant locos, with D8229 leading, inside the New Shed in 1971 – apologies for the quality! *(Author's Coll)*

By 1971 only three Class 20s remained allocated to Stratford; D8030 (seen here leading outside the DRS), D8055, second in line and D8056 at the back, still carrying green livery with full yellow ends. The two blue examples had tablet catcher recesses in the cab sides; a leftover from their earlier days in Scotland. I was disappointed to find that all three had moved away when I started work at Stratford in 1973. In a 40 year career I never worked on a Class 20 once. *(Author's Coll)*

My regular pilgrimages to Stratford were well rewarded, as shown here on 18th April 1972. The Class 24s became exceedingly rare after the mid-1960s, when the class was reallocated to the North-West and Scotland. A small batch was allocated to Gateshead (52A) in Newcastle for the Tyne Dock – Consett iron ore trains where they were double-headed. Nearly all the Gateshead 24s (5102-5111) came to Stratford DRS for attention over a period of several months. This is No. 5109 (24109) in colour as opposed to the black and white version in Part 1. *(A. Nugent)*

About to make its last ever trip to be cut up is Class 23 Baby Deltic Bo-Bo 1100 H.P. No. D5905 alongside the DMU shed at Stratford in July 1973. It is coupled to the only ever blue example D5909, which ironically has the words "Save Me" written in the brake dust; a plea which fell on deaf ears. Another member of this small class of 10 engines (D5901) survived until 1975 at Derby Research Centre, but this was cut up at Doncaster in 1977. A replica is being built at Barrow Hill Engine Shed near Chesterfield. *(Author's Coll)*

Class 03 0-6-0 204 H.P. No. 03168 (D2168) appears to have been shunted to the back of the New Shed and abandoned, but it was in fact very much still in use on 27th October 1974. The DMU inside the shed probably ousted the 03 so that the footpath at the other end was not fouled. This loco soldiered on until 9th August 1981, which is around the time that work was disappearing at Poplar docks. It was scrapped at Doncaster the same year. *(A. Meeks)*

The ironically named New Shed was once new, but by 1976 when this view was taken, it was one of the oldest structures on the depot. It was opened by the Great Eastern Railway in 1871 and as further sheds were added over the years, it still retained its title. Here we see Gloucester RCW and Derby built DMUs alongside a Toffee Apple Class 31/0 on the Accident Van road. The double storey building to the left was the old Tender Shops which once had an overhead crane inside. The former Loop line to Stratford Low Level passed between these two buildings. *(M. Lewis)*

At weekends, if you were lucky, there were sights like this for the intrepid explorer venturing into Stratford depot, as seen here on Saturday 24th April 1976. Meticulously lined up on the old inlet road are a collection of Class 31/0 "Toffee Apple" Brush Type 2s. Happy days indeed. *(M. Lewis)*

Rarely would photographers venture to the back of the DRS and capture trains on the High Meads loop line, as depicted here on 4th March 1978. Class 31 "Toffee Apple" Brush Type 2 No. 31019 (D5519) waits for the signal to enter Temple Mills yard with a mixed freight. The Freightliner terminal forms an interesting background and the 08 diesel shunter is working in the Stratford International Freight Terminal (SIFT). This view would be impossible today, as the High Meads loop is completely encased in a tunnel. *(M. Lewis)*

LONDON'S EAST END DIESELS

The stirring sight and sound of a pair of Class 40 English Electric 1Co-Co1 2000 H.P. locos on a frosty morning outside the DRS on 21ˢᵗ January 1978 is quite a heart warming spectacle. That was the joy of Stratford; you never knew what was going to appear overnight and the sound of a "Whistler" would give away its presence from afar. The locos are 40049 (D249) on the left and 40085 (D285) on the right. *(M. Lewis)*

A Class 43 High Speed Train (HST) power car No. 43060 minus its bogies sits inside the DRS on 18ᵗʰ June 1978. No less than 197 were built between 1975 and 1982 and they continue in service at the time of writing. Capable of 125 mph in everyday service and more in reserve, they are the main form of motive power for several of today's train operating companies (TOCs). Originally fitted with the 2250 H.P. Paxman Valenta engine, the whole class has since been re-engined with the more reliable Paxman 12RP200L unit. *(M. Lewis)*

The first of Stratford's three Open Days was on 14th July 1979, when the sun shone and life was a lot less stressful. The fitters at Finsbury Park depot had only just applied the white window surrounds to iconic Class 55 Co-Co 3300 H.P. 'Deltic' No. 55015 (D9015) "Tulyar" two days previously. Drawing huge crowds, the event was a great success. It gave members of the public a real chance to see the inner workings of the railway and motive power up close. "Tulyar" was withdrawn in 1982 but fortunately, it is one of the six preserved examples.

Looking at the external condition of 31015 (D5515) at Stratford Open Day in July 1979, one would expect that there was still life in this 30A stalwart. In fact, it was withdrawn from service just one year later, as traffic patterns were changing for the worse. By November the same year, its fate was sealed; 107 tons of locomotive turned into the same weight of scrap metal at Doncaster works. It is posed between two original LNER steam era tenders converted into snow ploughs, one of which is now part of a project to rebuild a Sandringham class 4-6-0. *(C. Stephens)*

Regular performers on the Stratford Low Level to North Woolwich route in the 70s and early 80s were the 1956 built Class 105 Cravens DMUs. This spruced up example is E50369 Motor Brake Second with a trailer car inside B shed on 10ᵗʰ June 1980. It was rare to see these units in here, but there were some jobs which were much easier to achieve because of the platform access which was not available in the railcar shed. *(B. Daniels)*

"Toffee Apple" Class 31/0 No. 31007 (D5507) stands on the site of the former Jubilee steam shed in August 1976. Even in the diesel era, these three roads were referred to as '3, 4 and 5 steam'. This loco entered service in April 1958 and only lasted until November 1976. It was cut up at Doncaster in 1978. *(A. Meeks)*

It was quite a juggling act by Stratford's Running Foreman to find room for all the locos to be stabled at weekends. Here we see all the former 'steam' roads gradually filling up on Saturday 24th April 1976. It was not unusual for the Foreman to come into the mess room and ask crews to get a loco out of the middle of a line up. All the locos had to be started up from cold, then we had to wait for the air to build up before they could be shunted around; this could take an hour, as they all had to be put back again afterwards. *(M. Lewis)*

A railway modeller would be proud to achieve this standard of weathering on a model. The real thing stands outside Stratford DRS in 1980. The English Electric Type 4 1Co-Co1 2000 H.P. locos (Class 40) have a huge following and no less than seven have been preserved. They lasted until 1985 in regular service. This is 40199 (D299), the last member out of 199 built. Always an Eastern Region loco, it was withdrawn on 14th June 1982 after fire damage and was cut up at Doncaster the following November. *(Author)*

Some of the rare visitors to Stratford DRS came in for wheel turning as one of the only wheel lathes in the London area was situated here. Today, the same work is carried out at Ilford Car Sheds and steam locos have been seen at Ilford in recent years. This is a Western Region Class 121 "Bubble Car" Pressed Steel unit No. W55022, built in 1960, waiting outside the DRS in the early 1980s. Out of the 16 built, 11 are preserved and one unit is still in service with Chiltern Railways. *(Author)*

Far from its usual stamping ground of working Teeside freight trains is Class 37 No. 37015 (D6715) from Thornaby depot on 12th April 1981 inside the DRS. Other locos under repair are Classes 47, 40 and 31/0. Judging by the gaping hole in the roof, the engine from 37015 has been removed. *(M. Lewis)*

A Stratford Open Day view taken on 11th July 1981 showing 47158 (D1751) "Henry Ford". This engine was named at Dagenham Dock by Mr. P. Hughes, the Vice-President of the Ford Motor Co. four days previously. The loco was reclassified Class 47/4 and renumbered 47634 in 1985. It was withdrawn in 2004. Behind the 47 is one of the best attractions; Class 55 Deltic Co-Co 3300 H.P. No. 55021 (D9021) "Argyll & Sutherland Highlander". *(Author's Coll)*

This was the last of Stratford's Open Days in August 1983, when the public was given the freedom to explore the depot and the repair shops. Classes of loco on display included from left to right, 47, 86, 37, 50, 41, 56 and 58. Several other diesel classes were represented out of view. On the left is the preserved steam loco "Britannia". Many thousands of enthusiasts from all over the country attended this event. *(Author's Coll)*

A regular sight at Stratford outside the New Shed would be a locomotive, often a Class 31 or 37 seen here, on Accident Van standby duty. The 75 ton crane was kept inside the shed and the loco could be started up and be on its way within about 15 minutes of getting a call to an incident. The crane was crewed by fitters who were 'on call' and lived close to the depot. 37215 (D6915) is seen in the winter of 1984. *(Author)*

Stratford's workshop painters were always kept busy. The trademark white roof applied to many Stratford engines was not always popular with the BR hierarchy, but then Stratford rarely conformed and its loco crews were equally rebellious, especially when it came to disputes with management. Class 31/0 Brush Type 2 "Toffee Apple" A1A-A1A No. 31005 poses at the back of the shed after having the full treatment along with an identical classmate, prior to working a special train in the late 1970s. *(P. Manley)*

This looks like the result of some horrible accident, but is in fact quite innocent. Class 31 No. 31122 (D5540) caught fire at Stonebridge Park on 8th January 1987 and was deemed to be beyond economic repair. The locomotive was one of only about a dozen Class 31s that were cut up at Stratford. Any reusable parts being stripped off first, the locomotive was slowly dismembered. The cab is seen here sitting on a Freightliner wagon outside the Diesel Repair Shop on 28th July 1987. *(A. Meeks)*

The sheer variety of locomotives found at Stratford was largely due to the skills of the fitters working in the Diesel Repair Shops, who seemed to turn their hand to the most obscure machines. Class 33 BRCW Type 3 1550 H.P. No. 33118 (D6538), allocated to both Hither Green (73C) and Eastleigh (70D) during its career, awaits attention alongside the DRS on 8th November 1988. Behind it is Class 31 No. 31280. *(A. Meeks)*

The former glory days of Class 40 No. 40092 (D292) are nearly over. This view was taken on 27th July 1983. The loco had been withdrawn on 28th November 1982 and was stored at Stratford from December 1982 until March 1984. It was moved to Temple Mills Yard on 28th March 1984 for re-railing tests and again on 5th June for breakdown tests. It was moved to Reading the same day and onto Swindon Works where the scrapman performed his dirty deed. Behind the 40 is Class 25 No. 25177 (D7527). *(A. Meeks)*

Stratford fitters and painters were very proud of their named Class 47s. This is 47582 "County of Norfolk" standing outside B shed in the early 1980s. The naming ceremony took place at Norwich station on 24th August 1979. It started life as D1765 in 1964 and took the TOPS number 47160 in March 1974, becoming 47582 in February 1981. It then became 47733 "Eastern Star" in 1995 and the original nameplates were sold off. It was scrapped in 2008.

British Railways Derby built Type 4 1Co-Co1 2500 H.P. No. 46021 (D158) looks rather the worse for wear after suffering collision damage in 1983. The Class 46 (D138–D193) locos were virtually identical to the Class 44 (D1–D10) and 45 (D11–D137) "Peaks" with the exception of Brush electrical equipment rather than the Crompton Parkinson components in the earlier members of the class. They were well liked by crews and enthusiasts, and today there are 17 examples in preservation. This view was taken on 27th July whilst the loco was in store at Stratford. It was cut up at Swindon in 1985. *(A. Meeks)*

This is Stratford Freightliner terminal in June 1990, where the mighty Class 90 electric loco is marooned without the assistance of the humble Class 08 diesel; in this case, the specially painted 08833 (D4001), normally used for the Liverpool Street pilot. Class 90 Bo-Bo 5000 H.P. locos were built between 1985 and 1990 with 50 eventually in service. This is No. 90040 waiting to be hauled under the wires – overhead wires and overhead cranes don't mix! The terminal closed in 1994. The last two daily services were to Crewe and Dagenham cold store. *(Author's Coll)*

This 47 started out in life during 1964 as D1616, originally allocated to the Nottingham depot Toton (16A). It was one of the earliest examples to be fitted with ETH and became 47480 under TOPS in November 1973. Considering its early career, it was appropriately name "Robin Hood" in November 1979. It was renumbered 97480 in September 1988, then again in July 1989 to 47971, so only carried this number for a few months. Pictured at Stratford on 23rd February 1989, it was withdrawn in May 2000 and cut up a year later. *(A. Meeks)*

If you had the good fortune to be sitting in the mess room at Stratford, sometimes the peace and quiet would be interrupted by a very unusual sound. The sound of twin Napier Deltic engines running is unmistakable; that 3300 H. P. unleashed is one of the most stirring sounds imaginable to any Deltic fan. By good fortune our photographer had his camera too, as preserved Class 55 Type 5 Co-Co No. D9000 (55022) "Royal Scots Grey" visits the depot in May 1999. *(A. Grimmett)*

A mid-1960s scene recreated almost to perfection, as 31110 (D5528), 37350 (D6700) and 47004 (D1524) are lined up alongside the shed to commemorate the closure of the depot on 1st July 2001. Fortunately, all the withdrawn, derelict and graffiti covered locos and their modern replacements were kept out of view. R.I.P. Stratford Depot 1871-2001. (A. Grimmett)

A Class 125 Derby built DMU more used to trundling up and down the Lea Valley line is found heading past Barking flyover on its way to Fenchurch Street in 1968. The lines on the flyover heading towards Woodgrange Park enabled freight traffic to and from Ripple Lane, Dagenham, Purfleet and Tilbury to by-pass the former junctions at the east end of Barking station unhindered. It opened in 1960 and took three years to build. *(B. Pask)*

Class 45 1Co-Co1 2500 H.P. No. D80 (45113) runs west through Barking in the early 1970s light engine. This was a BR Crewe built loco introduced in 1960 and first allocated to Derby (17A). The loco was renumbered 45113 in October 1973 and survived until 1988, being cut up at MC Processors Glasgow in 1990. It is seen returning to Cricklewood, having worked a freight to Ripple Lane. *(P. Scoote)*

Having just run round its train of 16 ton mineral wagons full of scrap, Class 31 No. 5626 (31202) is about to leave a very misty and murky Barking on its way to the goods yard at Upton Park in the early 1970s. This was a regular Stratford turn starting from Temple Mills, and the only remaining freight train running over the section from Barking towards Fenchurch Street at that time. *(P. Scoote)*

Probably the only time that a High Speed Train (HST) visited Barking, was the occasion of the London Tilbury & Southend Railway Centenary celebrations on 1st March 1980, when a special set ran from Liverpool Street to Southend Central to mark the event. It is seen heading east through the station with an 'elaborate' wooden headboard. *(Author's Coll)*

The huge amount of Thameside freight traffic in the late 1950s necessitated a dedicated diesel depot in order to save a large number of light engine movements to and from Stratford, the parent depot. Only light maintenance was carried out here. Ripple Lane opened in 1960 to coincide with the remodelled adjacent hump yard. At weekends it was often packed with locomotives as seen here in 1976. The hump yard was later flattened and the Freightliner terminal was built on the site. The depot closed in 1993. *(M. Lewis)*

A rather grubby looking Brush Type 2 No. D5652 (31226) speeds through Dagenham Dock with a Thames Haven bound oil tank train in April 1970. The signalman here had one of the busiest boxes on the line, as the level crossing is on the main route into Ford's car plant and huge queues of traffic and workers were a frequent sight. Ford's also boasted a huge internal railway system using several ex-BR 03 and 04 diesel shunters. *(G. Wareham)*

The Romford to Upminster branch line is captured on the 1st March 1965, as a Met-Cam DMU calls at Emerson Park Halt. This station retained this time-warp like appearance for another decade before it was modernised. The train is heading towards Upminster; spare a thought for the driver's that ply their trade up and down this line for a whole shift. Just eight minutes from end to end and back again; Ad infinitum! *(D. Fairhurst)*

The same DMU is captured later in the day as it leaves Upminster for Romford. The branch line was opened by the London Tilbury & Southend Railway in 1893 with a separate station at Romford on the opposite side of South Street to the GER station. The LT&SR ticket office closed in 1934 and the station was linked to the main station via a footbridge. *(D. Fairhurst)*

Looking far too clean to be working an engineering train, Class 47 No. 47674 sits in Leyton Ballast Depot in June 1994. The amount of renumberings that some locos underwent was often bewildering. This one started out as D1972 in 1965, then became 47271 under TOPS in 1974, 47604 in 1983, 47674 in 1991 and finally 47854 in 1995. It was named "Women's Royal Voluntary Service" in 1988 and carries the nameplates here. It was only allocated to Stratford from March 1994 for 12 months. The yard closed shortly afterwards to make way for the controversial M11 Link road which opened in 1999. *(A. Grimmett)*

This is such a rare view that it is worthy of inclusion here in this book of diesels! LNER designed Thompson Class B1 4-6-0 No. 61253 sits next to the brake van road in Temple Mills yard in 1961. The locomotive is in steam and was allocated to Norwich (32A) at this time. Within 12 months, steam would vanish from the whole of East Anglia. Fortunately, an 08 diesel shunter has just scraped into the picture and saved the day. *(Author's Coll)*

A view of Temple Mills marshalling yard in 1960 as Class 15 BTH No. D8229 leaves with a freight bound for Feltham on the Southern Region. This yard consisted of almost 50 sidings at its peak and the area to the right is Temple Mills Wagon Works. This view is taken from the Control Tower with its panoramic view over the whole yard. To the right, the River Lea can just be glimpsed. *(Author's Coll)*

Class 45 "Peak" 1Co-Co1 2500 H.P. No. D123 (45125) arrives on the hump reception roads with 8E25 off the Midland Region in April 1970. This was a Toton (Nottingham) allocated locomotive, so would have been a rare 'cop' for an East End trainspotter! Two 08 hump pilots are in the background. Two pairs of pilots were needed at this time to cope with the amount of traffic. The footbridge across the tracks here survives, but the only view today is of Orient Way carriage sidings. (G. Wareham)

It never ceased to amaze me what would turn up next in Temple Mills Marshalling Yard. The added advantage of being on the footplate and having a camera is evident here, as an unidentified Class 52 C-C 2700 H.P. "Western" moves slowly towards its train, guided by the Yard Master on the ground in 1972. The added bonus of a Class 33 BRCW Type 3 Bo-Bo 1550 H.P. sitting outside the shunters' hut is a rare combination of East meets West meets Southern! (Author's coll)

Class 31/0 "Toffee Apple" No. 31005 (D5505) basks in the sunshine during a lull in proceedings at Temple Mills yard in June 1977. This loco was withdrawn in February 1980 and cut up at Doncaster the following month. This, along with several other images in this book, was taken by Andy Nash (ex-Stratford secondman), who I lost contact with for 35 years, only meeting up again in 2014, when he kindly loaned his superb unpublished slide collection for this book. *(A. Nash)*

Class 31 No. 31239 (D5666) arrives on the Hump Reception roads in 1979 with a freight from Whitemoor (March). We are looking north towards Lea Bridge. Over 100,000 tons of earth had to be removed from this area to level the yard in the 1990s. EWS briefly had a locomotive depot on this site and Orient Way carriage sidings (opening in 2008), now occupies this site. *(B. Daniels)*

Our photographer has ventured up one of the lighting towers! His adventure has paid off with a very rare panoramic view of Temple Mills looking towards Stratford in 1980. Like so many photos in this book, the photographer was a driver with the foresight to record everyday scenes. Just beyond the first cabin are the primary retarders. Operating the retarders was a highly skilled job relating to how heavy the wagon was and how far in the siding it was needed. On the left is the former West Yard, which has become very overgrown. Two 08 Hump Pilots survey the scene. *(A. Williamson)*

"Where's the blooming diesels gone?" Well, there is the front of an 08 pilot but you need a magnifying glass to see it! We often forget about the people that run the railways, but these three gentlemen were always kind enough to let the loco crews sit in the Hump Cabin during breaks in the shunting. We are looking north towards Lea Bridge in the summer of 1980. *(A. Williamson)*

Temple Mills had its own dedicated loco depot and servicing point, seen here in 1976 looking towards Stratford. It opened in 1961 and saved a lot of light engine movements to and from Stratford depot. By the late 1960s it was abandoned for loco servicing but continued to be useful for wagon repairs under cover. The adjacent sidings were used for wagons undergoing or waiting repair in Temple Mills Wagon Shops across the tracks. *(M. Lewis)*

Working on the Hump Pilots (2 pairs) or the two Manor Yard/End pilots in the 1970s meant that you would spend between 8 and 12 hours on the 08 diesel shunter, with perhaps the odd break between shunts when you would retire to the shunters' cabin. This was 'home' during these lengthy shifts. The brass control handles are the engine stop/start, forward/reverse, and the large handle is the power controller. On the right is the Westinghouse vacuum brake and the tiny stool we had to perch on. *(A. Nash)*

Class 31/0 "Toffee Apple" No. 31009 (D5509) leaves Temple Mills yard on 19th June 1975 and is about to pass Temple Mills West signal box which is just out of view to the right. Behind the photographer is Lea Bridge station which was still very much in use at this time. This photo is rather poignant for me, as I'm almost sure that I am the secondman gazing out of the cab window; I would have only been 18 at this time. I was not aware of this photo's existence until researching for material in 2014. *(M. Lewis)*

Lea Bridge station was a good vantage point to catch freight arrivals at Temple Mills from the Lea Valley and South Tottenham via the Tottenham & Hampstead Joint line, which was frequently used by inter-regional services, as seen here in April 1969. BR Sulzer Type 2 (later Class 25) Bo-Bo 1250 H.P. No. D5220 (25070) passes behind the station with a freight off the Midland on the Up Goods line. Lea Bridge goods yard is in the background. *(G. Wareham)*

A view from the signal box at Hackney Downs as Class 47 No. 47130 (D1721) hauling a failed Class 31 No. 31318 (D5852) on an Up Cambridge service, roars round the curve after passing through Clapton tunnels on 7ᵗʰ June 1980. Sadly, there are no regular loco hauled services over this line today. *(Unknown/Author's Coll)*

Copper Mill Junction signal box is seen when still functional in 1967. Signalling on the section of line between Temple Mills West and Brimsdown was transferred to Temple Mills West box in February 1969, which made this box redundant and it was demolished shortly afterwards. We are looking south towards Stratford as a Liverpool Street to Cheshunt Class 125 Derby built DMU meanders by. The two tracks in the foreground are the goods lines. *(G. Tonkin)*

Tottenham South Junction was a good vantage point to capture the rare inter-regional freight trains plying their trade to and from Temple Mills. Our photographer catches Class 33 BRCW Bo-Bo 1550 H.P. No. 33212 (D6597), the last member of the class, leaving the Lea Valley main line and rounding the curve towards South Tottenham station in August 1974 with a mixed freight for the Southern. Rather sadly, Norman Cadge who took this and the following picture, passed away during the final stages of production. *(N. Cadge)*

Class 52 Western C-C 2700 H.P. No. D1056 "Western Sultan" approaches Tottenham South Junction from the South Tottenham direction with 8E38 for Temple Mills yard in August 1974. The Presflo, Conflat and 21T Grain wagons are just as nostalgic as the locomotive. This loco was withdrawn in December 1976 and cut up at Swindon in May 1979. Out of the 74 built, seven are preserved. *(N. Cadge)*

Just prior to the electrification of the Lea Valley line, we see a Class 125 Derby 3-car DMU coming to a stand at Northumberland Park in 1967. The leading vehicle carries a very early form of BR blue with half yellow ends, whilst the other two cars have retained their BR green. The train is a Cheshunt to Liverpool Street working. The Lea Valley line had tremendous character at this time but modernisation swept all vestiges of it away over the next two years. *(D. Fairhurst)*

A wonderful contrast of a rugged Ponders End Gas Works and a tranquil stream frame the Class 125 DMU in a mixture of BR blue and green liveries. The train is heading north approaching Ponders End station with a Liverpool Street to Cheshunt working in 1967. New overhead masts are starting to appear. *(D. Fairhurst)*

Ponders End station witnesses English Electric Type 3 Co-Co 1750 H. P. No. D6716 (37016) working the Up road 1K29 service for Liverpool Street in 1967. These hugely successful locomotives were ideally suited for the Cambridge and Kings Lynn services. We are looking north towards Brimsdown. *(D. Fairhurst)*

Admittedly, there's not a diesel in sight, but this wonderful image of the pre-electrification days at Ponders End was too good to omit. The goods shed, signal box and footbridge all have a good coating of grime and soot from thousands of passing steam and diesel trains over the decades. We are looking north in 1967, just prior to the modernisation. The signal box closed in1969. *(D. Fairhurst)*

The mixed fortunes of Ponders End station are all to apparent as a Class 125 Derby built 3-car DMU calls with a Cheshunt to Liverpool Street service on 5th April 1969. The line was opened for new electric services the previous month but clearly all was not well, as DMUs are still running. The piles of rubble in the background tell a sad tale; to the left was the original Northern & Eastern Railway station building from 1840. To the middle, an area is being cleared for new tower blocks. *(D. Fairhurst)*

A delightful pre-electrification view of an unspoilt Brimsdown on 29th August 1965. One of Stratford's Derby built Class 125 3-car DMUs in green heads towards Stratford with a stopping service from Cheshunt. The station still has a full complement of old BR dark blue signs and totems. Industry abounds and the power station cooling towers are to the right. The signalman has wasted no time in shutting the level crossing gates behind the train. (*D. Fairhurst*)

Brimsdown with a pair of unidentified Brush Type 2s in green heading south towards Temple Mills with a lengthy freight in September 1967. The fading paintwork of the signal box and gathering of vehicles in the goods yard brings back memories of a bygone era. The Scammell Scarab in the livery of a local builder's merchant is unusual. Over 60 Scarab's are known to be preserved. (*D. Fairhurst*)

A British Thompson-Houston BR Type 1 Bo-Bo 800 H.P. locomotive heads south through Brimsdown on 29th August 1965 with a short freight bound for Temple Mills Marshalling Yard. Pure unadulterated nostalgia. *(D. Fairhurst)*

Thankfully, the Lea Valley line had a stay of execution from the rampaging modernisation and electrification that had engulfed the Enfield and Chingford lines in the early 1960s. This view is taken at Waltham Cross & Abbey looking north on 15th October 1967 just prior to the electrification programme which would sweep away decades of history and old enamel signage from a previous era. The Class 125 DMU is on a Liverpool Street to Cheshunt service and comprises two blue power cars with a green liveried centre car. *(D. Fairhurst)*

I know that this is taking the London's East end theme a bit too far, but the train is heading that way! This image is just too good and merits inclusion. Furthermore, it might not get published elsewhere, which would be a real shame. We've come almost to the end of the Hertford East branch in 1961. Ware station has the unusual arrangement of a short single line on a double track branch line due to limited clearances. The Derby Class 125 unit is heading south just before the full electric services started. Lovely old BR dark blue enamel totem signs hang under the canopy. *(D. Fairhurst)*

Track lifting of the former Lower Edmonton Low Level goods yard is taking place as EE Type 3 Co-Co 1750 H.P. No. D6726 passes on the main line with a Cambridge to Liverpool Street service diverted off the Lea Valley on 27th June 1965. The train is approaching Lower Edmonton station, which has been known as Edmonton Green since 1992. Behind the photographer is the former Low Level station. We are looking north towards Edmonton Junction. *(D. Fairhurst)*

It is probably true to say that this is the one and only time that an English Electric Type 1 Bo-Bo 1000 H.P. Class 20 ever visited the long-closed Lower Edmonton Low Level station. Unfortunately, the occurrence is marred by the fact that the engine is at the head of the track lifting train in 1965. Although the station closed officially on 11th September 1939, it was frequently used up until the early 1960s for trains diverted off the Lea Valley at Angel Road, in order that engineering work could take place. The local kids have dragged their Mum's and Dad's down to the station to see what is making that infernal whistling noise! *(D. Fairhurst)*

The Railway Correspondence & Travel Society (RCTS) ran their East London No. 5 Railtour on 6th June 1981 formed of a 4-car Cravens DMU. It visited Poplar, North Woolwich and is seen here at Enfield Town where the lucky participants are roaming around taking in the delightful scenery! In the sidings we can see one of the regular Class 305/1 (AM5/1) EMUs which were used on the Enfield, Chingford and Hertford East services. *(Author's Coll)*

Class 60 No. 60079 "Foinaven" stands at the rear of an engineering train at Forest Gate on 26th January 2003. The Mainline freight liveried loco is one of several in the class which were named after Scottish mountains; modern day Peak's perhaps? *(A. Grimmett)*

This is the only picture I've ever seen of a diesel shunting in Manor Park goods yard. Class 31 No. 31199 (D5623) performs its tasks amongst the heaps of coal and Bedford trucks in 1979. The yard closed shortly after this view was taken by a member of the train crew. *(G. Weller)*

Roaring past Ilford Flyover amidst the tangle of the overhead wires and stanchions is Class 47 No. 47164 with the Union Jack livery applied for the Queen's Silver Jubilee in 1977 on a Norwich to Liverpool Street service. This was the last year that I was a secondman on these jobs, so I got to drive them on a daily basis (unofficially of course), but that was how we learned our trade. We are looking east towards Ilford station. On the left is a footpath next to the cemetery which is where I spent many happy hours as a kid. *(G. Silcock)*

D. Wickham & Co. of Ware in Hertfordshire built only five Class 109 2-car DMUs between 1957-9. Being non-standard, maintenance was a problem and they were sold back to Wickham, who then sold four units to Trinidad. The one remaining unit, DB975005 (E50416) and DB975006 (E56171) is seen here passing Ilford Station signal box in 1970. It had been converted at Doncaster in 1967 to become the General Managers Saloon. After withdrawal in the early 1980s, it was preserved and can now be found working on the Llangollen Railway. *(Author's Coll)*

One of the only places left within the area covered in this book, where it is still possible to see a working 08 diesel shunter is at Ilford Car Sheds. One is in regular use and another is kept as a standby. Much of the shunting carried out is out of the public gaze but our photographer is a railwayman, so has access to all areas. A Class 312 EMU driving trailer No. 724 is being shunted by 08573 (D3740) on 7th January 2004. The shunting barrier wagon on the left was formerly a Conflat wagon. *(A. Grimmett)*

Thankfully there is still some classic traction running around the old East End, but it is confined to test trains, rail head treatment trains and the occasional special. The Class 47 No. 47793 on the Serco test train seen passing Ilford Car Sheds in the spring of 2003, has a long association with Stratford; in a past life it was 47579 "James Nightall GC" from 1981 until 1995. It was also named "St. Augustine" from 1996 until Feb 2003, then "Christopher Wren" from Feb 2003 until Dec 2004; the name carried here. It survives in preservation as 47579 "James Nightall GC" (one of the Soham wartime disaster hero's) and can be found at Mangapps Farm Railway Museum in Essex. Alongside is Class 31 No. 31601 "Bletchley Park Station", formerly known as D5609 and 31186. *(A. Grimmett)*